Little
Audrey

Little Audrey

Ruth White

Farrar Straus Giroux
New York

Copyright © 2008 by Ruth White
All rights reserved
Distributed in Canada by Douglas & McIntyre Ltd.
Printed in the United States of America
Designed by Jonathan Bartlett
First edition, 2008
1   3   5   7   9   10   8   6   4   2

www.fsgkidsbooks.com

Library of Congress Cataloging-in-Publication Data
White, Ruth, date.
    Little Audrey / Ruth White.— 1st ed.
        p.   cm.
    Summary: In 1948, eleven-year-old Audrey lives with her
father, mother, and three younger sisters in Jewell Valley, a coal
mining camp in Southwest Virginia, where her mother still
mourns the death of a baby, her father goes on drinking binges
on paydays, and Audrey tries to recover from the scarlet fever
that has left her skinny and needing to wear glasses.
    ISBN-13: 978-0-374-34580-8
    ISBN-10: 0-374-34580-5
    [1. Country life—Virginia—Fiction.   2. Family life—
Virginia—Fiction.   3. Coal miners—Fiction.   4. Poor—Fiction.
5. Death—Fiction.   6. Virginia—History—20th century—
Fiction.]   I. Title.

PZ7.W58446Li 2008
[Fic]—dc22

                                                    2007029310

For Yvonne and Eleanor

The White family in 1944
Top row: Mommy with baby Betty Gail, Audrey
Bottom row: Eleanor, Ruth Carol, Yvonne

To My Readers

Much of the following story is true. If you see similarities to some of my previous books, it is because I have often drawn from real life to create my fiction.

In this book I have written about a time of great trauma in my family. I have used the voice of my oldest sister, Audrey, who was eleven at the time, to tell the story in her own words as she might have done then. Audrey died in 1993, so I have had to imagine her thoughts and feelings, much of the dialogue, and a few of the characters, but the basic events are true, and the most important characters were very real.

Mommy died also, in 2001. My sisters Yvonne and Eleanor helped me with the details of the story. We are the only ones now who remember how it was for us in an isolated coal mining camp in southwest Virginia in 1948.

Little
Audrey

1

It is a golden day in May 1948. The air fairly sparkles with sunshine. The sky is hard and glassy like a marble, and the new green of the hills is emerald. I am eleven years old, but in November I will be twelve, which is nearabout grown up. I am in the sixth grade, and I am walking home from school with Virgil. He is the new boy, just moved here from Kentucky.

"I like the color of your eyes, Audrey," he says to me.

"Which one?" I ask him.

"What do you mean?"

"Which eye?"

He is stumped.

"One of my eyes is blue, Virgil, like my mommy's and daddy's and the three little pigs', but the other eye is gray like nobody else's in the family."

He leans in close to look under my glasses. I don't know another kid in the world besides me who has to wear glasses. Mommy says it was the scarlet fever. It settled in my eyes. And it made me skinny.

Virgil is so near, I can smell the starch in his clothes. His mommy keeps him nice.

"Well, I'll be a monkey's uncle," he says. He's always throwing in a monkey somehow or other. Virgil says he likes animals better than most anything, but he has a peculiar soft spot for monkeys, even though he's never met one face-to-face.

"Which color do you like, Virgil?"

"Both of them. They're pretty. You're pretty."

That makes me smile. Virgil is nice to everybody. He knows a hundred jokes, and all the girls want to hang around him, but he likes me better than anybody else. He wanted to walk home with me, not with Hazel or Grace or any of the boys either.

We are walking on the dirt road in Jewell Valley, which is a coal camp in southwest Virginia. Jewell Valley is set in a deep valley with mountains rising up on either side of us.

There's a creek at the base of one mountain. The road is in the middle, and a row of houses is against the other mountain. The black winter mud is dried up on the road. Soon it will be time for the black dust. But it's nice now, without mud or dust.

"What—who's the three little pigs?" Virgil wants to know.

"My sisters. Yvonne is eight, Eleanor is seven, and Ruth Carol is six. I call them the three little pigs 'cause they hog all the food."

"I know what you mean," he tells me. "I have a little brother."

"Just one?"

"One's enough."

He's right about that. I have wondered lots of times why Mommy and Daddy just kept on getting babies even after they knew there was not enough of anything to go around.

"Speaking of pigs," Virgil says, "do you know what happened when the pigpen broke?"

"What?"

"The pigs had to use a pencil!"

We laugh. "I like you, Virgil," I tell him. "You're funny and smart."

He glances behind us.

"Uh-oh, here they come," he says, and I know he's talking about Thurman and Ron Keith, two real mean boys from our class. I take a deep breath.

"Well, if it ain't Little Audrey and the prissy boy," Thurman calls out.

We turn to look at them, but go on walking.

"What do y'all want?" I say. They are right on our heels.

"We got a dare for you, Little Audrey," Ron Keith says.

It's always a dare with these two. I dare you this. I dare you that. In Jewell Valley, when you get dared to do something, you have to do it. There's no way out of it. 'Cause if you don't do it, you will be made fun of for the rest of your life.

But after you do the dare, the one who dares you has to do it, too. Last summer Thurman and Ron Keith dared me to rub poison ivy on my face. And like a moron I did, then they did. A few days later we were all laid up with our eyes swole shut.

"You two are exasperating!" I say. It's a word our teacher, Miss Stairus, uses all the time, and I adore her with all my heart. Everybody adores her, even mean boys like Ron Keith and Thurman.

"You kids are exasperating," Miss Stairus will say to us, but she is smiling when she says it. I like the way she calls us kids instead of young'uns, like all the other grownups do.

But when that word *exasperating* comes from me, it tickles Ron Keith's and Thurman's funny bones.

"His—ass—what?" Ron Keith hoots, and they go into hysterics.

Did I say they also have dirty minds? Well, they do.

"You're not so smart!" Ron Keith says. "Fancy words don't make you smart!"

"Smarty, Smarty had a party!" Thurman chants. "And nobody came but Smarty, Smarty!"

He thinks he's being clever, but everybody has heard that old rhyme a thousand times.

"What's the dare?" I say.

"The prissy boy has to do it, too," Thurman says, and punches Virgil pretty hard on his arm.

They grin at Virgil, waiting for an answer. Virgil's face goes red. I don't think he's used to bullies. Maybe they didn't have them in Kentucky.

And now I don't know what has got into me. I stop in the middle of the road and start acting like John Wayne. "Spit it out! What's the dare?"

Everybody stops walking. We face each other.

"Climb the water tank," Thurman answers.

"That's no dare!" I holler. "I've done it lots of times. Everybody has."

"At night?"

I say nothing.

"All the way to the top?"

"And walk around the rim?"

They grin some more. Both of them have rotten teeth right in the front where you can see them plain.

I turn to look at the giant silver tank built high on the hillside. It glints in the sun, and my eyes burn. The tank holds the water supply for the coal camp, and kids like to play there. No one has ever gone more than halfway up the thousand steps. But I exaggerate. One hundred steps maybe.

"You're a skarity-cat," Ron Keith says to me.

"I am not! I'll climb your old water tank, and I'll do it at night, too."

Maybe I am addled in the head.

"When?"

"When I get good and ready, that's when!"

Ron Keith winks at Thurman. "She won't do it."

"I will so do it!"

But my mouth has gone dry.

"And what about you, prissy boy?" Thurman says to Virgil.

Virgil says nothing, and we hurry away. We can hear Ron Keith and Thurman following us, hollering and laughing, calling Virgil a baby.

Then they reach their house and go in. In Jewell Valley all the houses are exactly alike—square brown wooden boxes—but we know which one is which. Thurman lives in the right side of the seventh house, and Ron Keith lives in the left side. That's how these houses are made—two families in each one, with a wall down the middle to keep you private. But let me tell you something: voices go right through that wall.

Me and Virgil walk on. I don't say anything. My

mind is back there hanging on to that conversation with Ron Keith and Thurman.

"We don't have to be scared of them," Virgil says to me.

"I'm not scared," I lie.

"I bet we can outsmart them," he says.

I don't say anything.

"In fact, I bet a monkey could outsmart those two," he goes on.

He's got me laughing now, and I am thinking how different Virgil is. He's not like anybody else I know. Something surprising comes out of his mouth every time he opens it.

We come to the eleventh house, where I live in the right side. Mr. and Mrs. Church live with their teenage son, Dwight, on the left side. Our front door is open to let in the spring, and we can hear chattering from in there.

"Is that your mommy and your sisters talking?" Virgil asks me.

"Just my sisters," I say. "Mommy's away."

"Away? Where at?"

Away is not the right word, I reckon. Mommy is not really gone, but she might as well be a million miles from here. She's all caught up in her own secret world inside her head.

That's too hard to explain, so I just say, "I'll be seeing you, Virgil."

"Can I walk you to school tomorrow?" he says.

"Tomorrow is Saturday."

"Oh, I mean Monday. But I'll probably see you before then."

I nod my head and wave. He waves and goes on up the road to the last house in the row.

2

Our living room has some shabby furniture in it that Mommy and Daddy got secondhanded before I was borned. I pass through there and find the three little pigs eating oatmeal at the table in the next room. Yvonne and Eleanor get out of school before me, and Ruth Carol don't go to school yet.

My sisters got all the pretty parts of Mommy and Daddy, and I got all the not-so-pretty ones. They got Daddy's blond hair, but my hair is brown like Mommy's. They got Daddy's strong white teeth, while I got Mommy's eggshell ones.

My sisters are petite like Mommy, while I am

tall and lanky like Daddy, and right now I am thin as a poker. My sisters have teeny feet like Mommy, and I have clodhoppers like Daddy. They are also cute in the face like Mommy, but everybody says I got Daddy's plain face.

Mommy is standing, staring out the window, and rubbing Vaseline on her hands. I can tell by her eyes that she is not in there. She has been away for days. Mommy is just peculiar that way, and I don't remember a time when she was different. Something happens to trigger these spells, like some kind of bad news, or being reminded of a sad time in the past, or Daddy being meaner than usual. Most times I catch on to what the trigger is, but this time I didn't see it coming. I don't know what brought it on, or when she'll snap out of it, but she always does.

The room where we eat is not very big. The table is in it, and six chairs. There's the cabinet that holds our dishes. Mommy's sewing machine is by the window. And the stairsteps are in here, too. There are three steps, then a little landing, and you turn left and go up eight more steps to our two bedrooms.

Off this room there's an itty-bitty kitchen

where Mommy works. The cooking stove is in it, with a coal bucket beside it. On a wooden box is the water bucket and dipper, also the hand-worshing pan with a piece of soap in it. Under the window is the scrub board and worshtub for clothes and for taking baths. The skillets and kettles for cooking and the dishpan are all hanging on the wall.

Some people in the camp have a Frigidaire, but we don't. And nobody has water coming through pipes, but outside, between each house, there's a pump where the cold water comes down to us from the big water tank on the hill that Thurman and Ron Keith dared me to climb. If you want hot water, you heat it on the cooking stove. The toilets are outside. That's the way it is. I wisht things were different and better, but they're not.

Mommy has an older sister named Nancy, and she has a job in a casket factory way out in Roanoke. She's the only one in her family who left the county and went to live somewhere else. To get a better life, she said.

When she came to visit us one time, I heard her say to Mommy, "The man who made this coal camp orta be arrested."

I think it made Mommy feel bad to hear those words.

"It's better than no home a'tall," Mommy said to Aunt Nancy. "Besides, it's temporary."

She meant we won't live here forever. She's always saying that, but after three years, I'm starting to wonder.

Right now Yvonne is saying to me, "You know Mommy doesn't want you to play with boys. They are too rough."

She is the eight-year-old, and the most exasperating of the three little pigs. Her full name is Yvonne Marie and Daddy named her his own self, after two of the famous Dionne quintuplets. She thinks she's something. Mommy gave the rest of us regular names.

"Virgil is not rough. He's real smooth," I tell her.

I find a bowl and put a glob of oatmeal in it. There is no milk. There is no sugar.

Mommy is still gazing out the window, but I don't think she sees anything out there.

"Mommy, can I go to the store?" I ask her.

"Umm . . . ?" she says without turning around.

"We need some milk," I say.

"We've used all the scrips," she says.

That's how you buy food in a coal camp: with scrips instead of money. They have *Jewell Valley Coal Company* stamped on them. You take them to the company store to buy what you need, or trade them in for real money if you want to spend it somewhere else. But if you're like us and don't have a car, you have to get your food right here in the camp. Most times we use all the scrips up before the week is out. The company store gives us nickels and dimes for change, and Mommy saves them for going to the show.

"Well, it's payday," I tell her. That means Daddy will bring home more scrips from work.

"It'll be all right," she mumbles. She says that a lot. It's just a habit. Then she goes back to her own world. I don't know where her world is at, or who is in it. I only know she goes in there when she can't stand us no more. I know it's the truth 'cause I do it, too.

In my world there is Mr. Rochester and Jane Eyre. She looks exactly like Miss Stairus. They live in a mansion called Thornfield, and it is full of servants who bring them good things to eat any time they want it. And they don't have to dig in the coal mines for it. They have a dog named Pilot. He never gets mange, and nobody ever kicks him.

But at Thornfield, do you want to know the person who fascinates me the most? It's the crazy woman in the attic. They put her there 'cause she bites people and lights fires. But still I like her. I feel sorry for her. I wonder what made her crazy.

In the cabinet there is one can of Borden's evaporated milk with Elsie the cow on the front of it. I find the can opener, punch two holes in it, and pour it on my oatmeal. Ruth Carol is the six-year-old runt piglet. Sometimes I call her Runt Carol. Now she starts to squeal. She wants some Borden's, too, so I pour it on her oatmeal.

Her nose is runny, and I say to her, "Runt Carol! Wipe your nose on your petticoat!" But she don't.

"I heard another Little Audrey joke today," Yvonne says.

I groan. There's this little girl in the funnies named Audrey like me, and lately Little Audrey jokes have got to be more popular than the knock-knock ones. That's why mean people like Thurman and Ron Keith have started to call me Little Audrey. I hate these stupid jokes. They're not even funny.

"Little Audrey got lost on a desert island." Yvonne jumps right in there with a big grin on her face. "And a bunch of camels came along and kidnapped her."

"You mean cannibals," I butt in.

"Huh?"

"CAN-nibals kidnapped her. Not camels! I heard it a'ready!"

But that don't matter to Yvonne. She'll tell it just the same.

"Anyhow," she goes on, "they tied her to a tree and started their pot to boiling. Little Audrey knew they were going to make a stew out of her. She looked around at those cam . . . ibals. They were ugly and mean, and boy, were they hungry! She counted them. Nineteen. And Little Audrey just laughed and laughed, 'cause she knew all the time she was too little to make enough stew to go around."

That's what always happens in Little Audrey jokes. She gets into these hopeless situations, and still she finds something to laugh about.

Yvonne and Eleanor start to giggling then like that joke might really be funny or something. Then Ruth Carol joins in, even though she don't understand a word of it. I go on eating my cold oatmeal, wishing for the umpteenth time that I was an only child.

3

After we eat, we wander outside 'cause it's nice weather out there. Yvonne, Eleanor, and Ruth Carol go up on the hill behind our house and start making a playhouse by an old stump. They turn the stump into their kitchen table, and they lay out good things to eat on it.

I go up the road. Maybe I will see Virgil. And yes, there he is with a pretty little white-headed boy. They are damming up the creek for a wading hole.

"Hidy, Audrey," Virgil calls to me. "This is my brother, Earl."

"Hidy, Virgil. Pleased to meet you, Earl."

"My daddy's sleeping," Virgil says. "He works

on the third shift. Me and Earl were making too much noise, so Mommy told us to come outside in the sunshine."

I have my shoes on, so I can't go in the creek. But I watch them playing. The sun is warm on our heads, and the tiny blue snake doctors skim across the top of the water.

"My daddy works on the first shift," I say, and feel sorry for Virgil's daddy 'cause he has to work all night.

"Yeah, that's what my daddy wants to do. He don't much like third shift or anything else in Jewell Valley, and Mommy hates it."

"Why did y'all leave Kentucky and move here?"

Virgil shrugs. "Daddy couldn't make a living on the family farm. He heard there's good money in coal mining."

"I reckon he heard wrong," I say.

"When I grow up, I am going to be something else besides a miner or a dirt farmer," Virgil says. "I bet you can't guess what."

"No, I can't. What?"

"A doctor for animals. And I am going to have me a pet monkey."

Again he surprises me. Here I am thinking that

people who live like we do don't grow up to be doctors and such, do they? Important people like that come from somewhere else, from cities and places up North. But my pulse seems to quicken. Who says me and Virgil can't be somebody?

"I think maybe I would like to be a teacher!" I say breathlessly.

It's the first time that thought ever crossed my mind, but it seems like such a great idea.

"Yeah, you're smart. You'd make a fine teacher," Virgil tells me. "I bet you'd be as good as Miss Stairus."

I think it's the best compliment I ever got, and I feel my face flush.

"We're going to walk down to the store to buy pop in a paper cup. Wanna come along?" Virgil asks me.

"I guess so. But I can't buy anything."

"I'll let you have some of my pop," Virgil says.

He takes his brother's hand and leads him out of the creek.

When we walk past my house, I can tell that my sisters are all caught up in their playing and don't see me. If they did, they would holler and try to tag along with me and Virgil and Earl.

"Why don't you go barefooted like other young'uns?" Virgil asks me.

"Mommy says I have to wait till June."

"How come?"

"I've been sick."

"Oh, Earl had whooping cough. What were you sick with?"

I don't really like to talk about it. It makes me feel blue. So I say, "We all had colds, and Ruth Carol had the whooping cough, too."

"You just had a cold?" Virgil says. He is puzzled. And I think this boy is so fine, maybe I'll tell him everything.

"Well, no. See, a while after Christmas I got the tonsillitis, and then scarlet fever. That's a sickness that makes you feel so awful that you're afraid you're going to die, and then you're afraid you won't."

"Poor Audrey," Virgil says, with real sadness in his voice.

Ain't he the sweetest boy?

"After that I had my tonsils out," I go on. "I bled a lot, and Dr. Stein told Mommy it was touch-and-go there for a while. I don't know what he meant by that. I fell off something awful, and the doctor says I still need to put on six pounds.

"When I came home from the hospital, I had to miss school and lay in the bed for a long time. I didn't get back to school until last month, and just lately, if the sun comes out real hot, Mommy lets me go outside to play. But I can't go barefooted like y'all do."

We don't talk as we go by Thurman and Ron Keith's house, 'cause if they are in there, they might hear us and come out to pester us. But we don't see them. They are prob'ly up at the water tank.

We walk all the way to the end of the camp, where the company store is at. The movie theater is here, too, also the doctor's office and the bathhouse.

I look toward the west and see the monster coal tipple reaching to the sky. It's like a tall conveyor belt and that's where the miners haul the coal to after they dig it out of the ground. They put it in the tipple, where it's carried to the railroad cars that are waiting on the tracks below.

It's about four o'clock, and the miners are getting off their shift now. We see them coming toward us. They don't talk. They carry their dinner buckets and walk slow 'cause they are wore out.

They have carbide lights strapped to their heads, and one man has forgot to turn his off. I don't know if Daddy is one of the men. You can't tell one from the other 'cause they are covered with coal dust from head to toe. Their black-rimmed eyes squint in the sunlight.

They are going to the bathhouse, where there is real hot water and all the soap they want to scrub with, and Halo shampoo to get the coal dust out of their hair and ears. I wisht I had me some of that shampoo.

When we go in the company store, Virgil takes Earl's hand again. I think that's nice. I would hold Ruth Carol's hand sometimes if she was a good kid like Earl, but she's whiny and squirmy.

At the soda fountain, Virgil orders two Coca-Colas in the cup. I love pop, but I don't hardly ever get any. Virgil gives me two swallows of his on the way back up the road, but I just sip a little bit 'cause I don't want to be a pig.

At my house, Virgil says, "Hey, Audrey. What is invisible and smells like bananas?"

"What?"

"Monkey burps!"

4

When Daddy comes home, he's scrubbed to a shine, with his curly yella hair still wet from the bathhouse. He has on fresh clothes that he took with him to work this morning, and his dirty ones are in a bag for Mommy to worsh.

He goes right straight to the eating table. Mommy has fixed us soup beans and corn bread.

"Don't we have some onions or taters?" Daddy wants to know.

Mommy mumbles, "No."

Daddy grunts, pulls out some fresh scrips from his pocket, and tosses them on the table. I can see that he has real United States of America money in his pocket, too. That means he's already traded in some of the scrips for cash at the company store.

Mommy picks up the scrips right then and puts them in the cabinet under the saucers. She will have to wait till in the morning to go to the store, 'cause they close at five o'clock every day, including Sunday. She will try to make the scrips stretch out till next Friday.

We don't talk much during supper 'cause Daddy's not in the mood for it. When he don't talk, we don't talk. But when he feels like chatting with us, then we chat, too. That's the way it is.

Today he eats fast, then gets up and pushes back his chair.

"I'm going to see Mom and Dad," he says.

We knew this was coming. Nearly every Friday he begs a ride with somebody who has a car, and goes to a place outside of Jewell Valley. Usually that place is Granny and Poppy's house down the road a piece, at Whitewood. Daddy and Granny and Poppy drink liquor together and play cards with other people who are fun to be with. Mommy is no fun. I know, 'cause Daddy has told me so.

Mommy is picking at her food. I see that her hands are raw from scrubbing mining britches on a worshboard with lye soap. Sometimes her knuckles bleed.

"Daddy, can I go with you?" I blurt it out, then hold my breath.

I am Granny and Poppy's favorite grandbrat, as they say, and Daddy used to take me to see them lots of times. Granny would make over me and give me good things to eat. Sometimes she gave me puffs off of her Lucky Strikes. But when I got sick everything changed. I didn't get to go with Daddy anymore.

Daddy looks at me and hesitates for only a second.

"Not this time," he says, and goes out the door.

Then he pops his head back in to say, "But tomorrow y'all can come and watch me pitch my ball game. It's over yonder at the schoolhouse."

Daddy is the pitcher for the miners' baseball team. Everybody brags on how good he can pitch. When Daddy pitches, his team wins.

After he leaves, I get a lonesome feeling like I had when I was sick in the bed. I liked it at the hospital 'cause the nurses treated me kind and gave me ice cream. They were always there with me, or no more than a few steps away. Mommy and Daddy came twice to stand beside my bed, too bashful and backward to talk to the doctor or nurses.

But when I came home, I had to lay in the darkened bedroom by myself all day. Mommy would bring me food and put her hand on my for'd to see if I was feverish. Then she would go back down the stairsteps.

Ruth Carol and Eleanor have food all over their faces. I can't hardly stand to look at them. I stomp outside and hide in the toilet. I stay in there till the stink makes me gag. When I come out, I watch the last of the light sitting high on the hill-tops. The golden day is almost gone.

I go up on the side of the hill and set down beside the playhouse my sisters made. Their pretend food—sticks and rocks and weeds—is still on the stump. Down in the camp I can barely see some dirty young'uns playing in the dirt yards and the dirt road. I can see the coal piles beside the houses, and the outdoor toilets, and the water pumps standing in black mud where the water has sloshed out.

Then I close my eyes and wait for the image of Thornfield to appear on the back of my eyelids. For some reason this evening it is a long time coming.

5

I am under a sheet and blanket in my petticoat and step-ins. This is one good thing I have—a bed of my own. My sisters are in the same room, but they are all three together in another bed 'cause they pee the bed every night. They have to sleep with a rubber sheet under the real sheet. Mommy keeps a slop jar in here, but do you think they'll get up and use it? This whole room smells like pee, but I don't notice it much anymore.

The Sheetrock in this room was never finished proper. It was just hung up there, and left like that. I reckon a little kid with a pencil or a crayon can't resist decorating it. My sisters have nearabout covered all four walls with their pictures of girls in pink dresses and happy animals and food. There's a Hershey bar over there by the door that looks pretty much like the real thing.

The moon is so bright tonight, I can almost see the figures on the Sheetrock. Yvonne draws the best. Eleanor colors the best. Ruth Carol just makes messes. In daylight you can see her dirty fingerprints where she tried to copy what Yvonne and Eleanor did.

They are sleeping now, but I can't sleep. Lots of times I lay awake in the night with stuff on my mind. Then I can't get out of bed the next morning.

I know Mommy is still downstairs, but I can't hear her. I wisht I could go down there and talk to her about things, you know, about school and Miss Stairus and Virgil, and what to do about that mean Thurman and Ron Keith. But if I try to tell her stuff like that, she just says, "Oh, it'll be all right." That's like telling me I don't really have a problem. Or, if I do, she'd rather not hear about it.

What in the world am I going to do? Thurman and Ron Keith will aggravate the tar out of me till I set a time to meet them, and go to the tank. I am scared. No, it's not the dark. I never been scared of the dark. Not the woods either. I love the woods, night or day.

And you know what? I bet if you climbed the steps right close to daybreak, you'd see the prettiest sunrise from up there on top of that tank. So if I go, I will tell Thurman and Ron Keith I'll have to go just before daybreak.

What do I mean *if* I go? I *have* to go.

But how can I climb that tank and walk around the top edge? There's just a little bitty ledge up there. What if I fall in? I can't swim. I will drownd for sure. I bet the insides are slick and there's nothing to catch a holt of. Yeah, that's what I'm scared of.

This is a warm night. So why am I shivering? I slip out of bed, pull the blanket around me, and go to the head of the stairsteps, where I sit on the top one and peep through the banister to where Mommy's at. She is reading. I will always see her like this. Even when I am an old woman with clouds in my eyes and hair like the dust balls under my bed, I will see Mommy sitting with an open book under a circle of lamplight. It's a peaceful thing.

Mommy has an uncle who lives on the top of Compton Mountain, where she grew up, and he has a whole library full of important books. She goes there whenever she can get somebody to take her. Uncle Hannibal lets her borrow as many books as she can carry down off the mountain, 'cause she always returns them in good shape. She reads them all, and Daddy does, too. They are both working their way through Zane Grey right now. She said one time that it was books that brung her and Daddy together.

In the last year or so I have been reading the books, too. That's where I found *Jane Eyre*. I also read *Wuthering Heights* and *David Copperfield*, and *Great Expectations* and *Tess of the d'Urbervilles*, and others that were hard to read, but I read them over and over again. *A Girl of the Limberlost* was easier.

I watch Mommy's red hands turning the pages. Earlier in the evening she was squeezing Ruth Carol tight with her eyes shut, and I knew what Mommy was doing. She was pretending that Ruth Carol was the baby that died. She does it all the time. She holds Ruth Carol and closes her eyes and pretends. But Ruth Carol squirms away from her.

Mommy thinks she's the only one who remembers the baby, but she's wrong. Why, at this very moment I am taking her out of that secret place in my heart where I keep her. It's been almost four years since she died, and she was with us for only seven months, so my memories of her are underdeveloped, like little green fruits that never got ripe.

Her name was Elizabeth Gail. Ain't it the prettiest name? It's the name of a princess. We called her Betty for short—Betty Gail. She died of something called spinal meningitis. She got sick and couldn't hold up her little head. Some people come and carried her off to the hospital, but it was too late. And she died.

I do remember how her blue eyes lit up when she laughed. I spent more time with her than Mommy did. I could make her laugh out loud. And she had deep dimples. Now we have only a picture of her, and that's when she was four months old, and we were living at Buck Jewell's place down at Whitewood where Daddy worked in the mines there. We moved to Jewell Valley for the free house.

In the picture we are out in the yard at Buck

Jewell's, all of us, except for Daddy. You can see the house in the background. It's white. I wisht we had a white house now, and a bit of yard. Mommy looks pretty in the picture. She is wearing a dress of some dark color, with bulky shoulder pads. I wonder what happened to that dress.

But it's Betty Gail you see first and last in that picture. What a doll baby she was! And sometimes I think Mommy would trade all of us in to have her back, if she could.

But I must be crazy to sit out here on this hard cold step. I am going back to bed now. I pull my blanket behind me, and sigh real big as I climb between the sheets. I know Mommy will be going to bed soon.

"Git off of me!" Eleanor is hollering at somebody, prob'ly Ruth Carol.

Eleanor was born fifteen months after Yvonne and fifteen months before Ruth Carol. She is seven now, and normally the quietest one in the house. She just sucks her thumb and minds her own beeswax. But she sees everything. She don't miss a trick. Eleanor June is what Mommy named her, after Eleanor Roosevelt and also our Aunt June Compton, Daddy's only sister.

The other day Eleanor told me she has a sweet-heart at school. She said he chased her around the heating stove in their classroom one time. She calls him by his whole name—George Elmer McGaffy.

Now Ruth Carol is whimpering.

"Y'all shut up!" comes from Yvonne, and pretty soon they do shut up, and I drift off to sleep.

My dreams are tender for a long time. It's real late when they change, and I start hearing the baby cry. It's a sad, sad cry. She's lost, all alone, crying for Mommy. Or for me. Her little wails echo through my dreams, and I wake up. Oh, why did I have to take her out tonight? I knew once I did, I would not be able to put her away again. She's like that.

Now I hear something more real. It's Daddy stumbling up the stairsteps. I hear him fall. It sounds like he has fallen down all the steps.

Thump! Thump! Thump! And ker-thump!

I raise up and listen. He's groaning. Is he hurt? Mommy gets up. In the dark I can just barely see her outline at the head of the stairs outside my door.

"John Ed?" she says, but he don't answer. "John Ed, you all right?"

He moans and groans.

"You want me to help you up?"

He cusses. At least I think he's cussing. You can't make out a thing he says when he gets liquored up.

Mommy waits for a few seconds, then says again, "John Ed, you want me to help you?"

"G' on! Lea' me 'lone," he mutters.

And Mommy does just that. She leaves him alone and goes back to bed. I lay down. I don't hear anything from Daddy or Mommy. After while I sleep some more, but my dreams are muddy.

6

I get up and put on the same dress I wore yesterday. When I go downstairs, Daddy is sprawled
out on his back on the landing with his legs laying
up the steps. There is dried blood on his chin. He
is snoring. I have to step over him. I am careful
not to bump him.

The three little pigs are at the table eating cold
oatmeal again.

"Is Mommy gone to the store?" I whisper.

"Yeah," Yvonne says. "And she said to tell you
to make sure Ruth Carol puts on some clothes before she goes outside."

I give the runt an exasperated look, but I don't

say anything. Yvonne and Eleanor are dressed, but Ruth Carol is in her petticoat. She's bad to go outside and around the camp like that if you don't watch her. One time she went to visit the Wimmers in her step-ins and nothing else.

I don't think I will eat any oatmeal. I will wait for Mommy to come home. She will bring something else to eat besides oatmeal and beans.

Suddenly Daddy lets out a monster snore. He sounds like a great big old hog. Me and my sisters explode into giggles. We can't help it. Daddy raises up, looking wild-eyed and bushy-headed. I see the blood is all over his neck, too. He has busted some part of his face when he fell in the night.

"Huh!" he snorts at us. "Huh!"

And we don't laugh anymore 'cause we're scared to.

When he tries to get up, he puts me in mind of a downed cow thrashing its legs around. Finally he manages to get onto all fours, then holds on to the banister and pulls his body from the landing real slow. He nearly crawls up the stairsteps, and we hear him go into his and Mommy's bedroom and close the door.

After Ruth Carol eats, I take her upstairs. The

dress she wore yesterday has dribbles of food down the front, but I can't find a clean one, so I put the dirty one on her. Then I go outside with her right at my heels.

It's another clear spring day. Yvonne and Eleanor have disappeared. They are probably down the road playing with Emogene, one of their friends.

The clotheslines in the camp are full of britches and housedresses and diapers and underwear and school clothes. You can hear the May morning breeze whipping them around. They will be dry by noon.

I go into our toilet, and when I come out, I see that Ruth Carol has walked to the Churches' open kitchen window in their half of our two-sided house. There is a glass of water on the ledge with a set of false teeth in it. They belong to Mr. Church.

I like Mr. Church. One day last fall, his wife threw out a mess of apple peelings on the hillside, and Mr. Church caught Ruth Carol eating them.

"Give that young'un an apple!" he barked at his wife. And she did. She gave Ruth Carol a great big old red apple. I felt like going over there to that pile of peelings and eating a few of them myself. But I didn't.

Then I heard Mr. Church mumble to his wife, "That John Ed White orta be horse-whooped!"

That's when I pinched Ruth Carol and made her go on home. I know the pinch hurt, but she didn't bawl 'cause she was too busy with that apple.

Now Ruth Carol is looking at the false teeth in the glass on the window ledge. She has never seen such a thing before, and her eyes are big.

"Look at that!" she says to me. "The tooth fairy's gonna run out of pennies."

I see Mrs. Mullins in the house next to ours come out carrying a slop jar. Poor Mrs. Mullins. Her and Mr. Mullins both are as ugly as a mud fence. But they're nice to us. With her free hand she waves at me and Ruth Carol.

"Hidy, girls. It's a purty Saturday, ain't it?"

Then she takes the slop jar into her toilet to empty it.

I go out to the road, and see Mommy coming. She is loaded down with pokes, and I run to help her out. Ruth Carol comes, too, but she's too little to help. I take some of the pokes from Mommy. Mommy does not speak.

"Daddy got up and went to bed," I tell her.

She grunts.

"What did you buy to eat?" I ask her while I am fumbling around in one of the pokes.

I find a small bag of flour. A can of salmon. A jar of peanut butter.

"Oh, boy! Peanut butter!" I say.

"I want some!" Ruth Carol whines. "Give me some!"

We are going in the back door. We set our pokes on the table.

Ruth Carol grabs the peanut butter and tries to open the top. It's just a little jar. Mommy takes it from her and screws off the lid. I don't know why in the world she does that. She knows Ruth Carol will stick her dirty fingers in the jar. And she does. That makes me so mad.

"Give it to me!" I holler, and grab the jar from Ruth Carol. She lets out a bloodcurdling shriek.

"Audrey!" Mommy fusses at me. Like I'm the one screaming bloody murder. "Give it to her!"

I take a teaspoon and stick it in the jar.

"Just git out what you want on this spoon!" I tell Ruth Carol. "And don't put your dirty fingers in the rest of it."

Then I take the spoon myself and dip out a big dollop of peanut butter. I set Ruth Carol down at the table with it. She's happy. I put the jar up high on a cabinet shelf where she can't reach. Then I help Mommy put away the rest of the stuff.

A dozen eggs. We'll have to eat them all before Monday. One time the last two eggs in the bag were rotten, and Mommy took them back to the store, and the store lady said, "Mrs. White, don't you know you have to put eggs in the Frigidaire?"

And Mommy said, "We don't have a Frigidaire."

And the woman said, "Your tough luck."

A quart of milk. We'll drink it all today.

Six pork chops. We'll have them for dinner. A can of applesauce.

A chunk of salted side meat. A bag of navy beans.

A lump of white margarine wrapped in clear paper with an orange button. What you do is mash the bag around and around in your hands until the orange button turns the margarine yella.

I don't know why I am disappointed. Did I think there would be something different in the bags?

"I couldn't carry everything," Mommy says as

she pushes some scrips into my hands. "We still need potatoes and onions and cabbage."

I understand that she wants me to go back to the store and get these things for her. In a whisper I ask her can I get me a Brown Mule, which is a stick of vanilla ice cream covered with chocolate.

I am surprised when Mommy nods yes and does not even say get one for everybody. Maybe she's thinking about that six pounds I need to put on my bones.

I take a teaspoonful of peanut butter for myself and eat it. Then I go back outside and skip all the way to the store.

7

When Daddy gets up around one o'clock, he sets at the table with his head in his hands. He's got a big blue lip. Mommy feeds him strong black coffee, fried eggs, a pork chop, and biscuits and gravy. He does not say a word. Neither does she. After eating, he puts on his baseball T-shirt that says JEWELL VALLEY on the back, and goes out the door.

When he's gone, the rest of us set down at the table and eat. I dig in. It's so good! Yvonne and Ruth Carol dig in, too. Mommy eats like she's bored with it. Eleanor has to separate everything on her plate first before she can start. She can't stand to have her food touching.

At two o'clock, nearly everybody in the camp is at the schoolhouse. It's up the road a piece from the coal tipple. The three little pigs and me are standing around the edge of the playground watching the men warm up. Mommy has stayed home like always. Daddy is throwing the ball to the catcher. I don't hear anybody ask him about his fat lip.

My girlfriend Hazel comes to me grinning, and puts her arm around my waist. She's got fiery red hair and lots of freckles. She's a sweet girl. Her daddy is Red Nunley, one of my daddy's drinking buddies.

"I nearly forgot they were playing today," Hazel says to me.

"They play here every other Saturday," I say.

"What does that mean?" she asks me.

I'll say one thing about Hazel. She does not mind asking questions when there's a thing she can't understand. And I'm sorry to say there's plenty of things she don't understand, lots more than most folks. She looks up to me 'cause I read books.

"What does it mean?" she says again. "Every other Saturday?"

To be fair to Hazel, that expression really don't make a whole lot of sense, does it? Every other Saturday. Huh. Wonder who ever thought that up. And leave it to Hazel to worry on things like that.

One time I said, "Knock on wood!" and she asked me what it meant. Try explaining "knock on wood" to somebody who don't already know! Another time it was "more often than not."

While I am telling her what "every other Saturday" means, Eleanor commences pulling on my sleeve.

"Audrey, look at my eye," she says, and puts one finger underneath her right eye. "What's wrong with it?"

I look. Yeah, she's got the beginnings of a stye coming up there. It's a red bump with a little yella center right on her lower eyelid.

"Maybe a stye," I tell her, though I know there's no maybe about it. "Better go show it to Mommy."

Eleanor's about to cry. She don't like to have things wrong with her. One time she layed out of school 'cause she had pinworms. Mommy wouldn't take her to the doctor just on account of pinworms, so Eleanor went by herself. The doctor sent her home with this nasty yella medicine that we all had to take.

Now she leaves the playground to go to Mommy, and the game starts. The fellers from the other team look puny to me. Not one of them is tall like my daddy. And they can't hit a ball worth a dern. After while somebody hits a foul over on the hillside, and everybody has to wait for our fielders to find the ball. Daddy squats down in the dirt to wait.

"Audrey!" he hollers at me suddenly, and I nearabout jump out of my skin. "Audrey, go git me a dipper full of water!"

I go fast to the water bucket that sets on the schoolhouse porch. I scoop up a dipperful and run right out in the middle of the playground to Daddy. Everybody is watching, and I feel proud. I hope Virgil is here. I give the water to my daddy. He drinks it all in one big gulp. Then he wipes his mouth with the back of his hand, being careful not to hurt the blue lump.

He hands the dipper to me, and I ask him does he want some more. But he's done with me. Somebody has found the ball. I go and put the dipper in the bucket. Then I walk to where Hazel is at.

"Your daddy's a good pitcher," she says to me. She just says that 'cause she's heard other people say it. Hazel wouldn't know a good pitcher from a scarecrow. For that matter, neither would I.

But I say, "Thank you," just the same.

"That John Ed White couldn't pitch his way out of a paper poke!" I hear somebody else say, and I don't even have to turn around to know who it is. Nobody but Thurman would say such a thing about Daddy, and he just says it 'cause he's mean and jealous.

His words fly all over me, and without even thinking I whirl around and yell at Thurman, "Yeah? Why don't you say that to his face, then?"

Everybody around us has heard what he said, and what I said, too, and they all laugh. I am tickled to see Thurman's face go red. Then the warning bells go off in my head, and I say to myself, Wait a minute. Hold on there, Audrey Virginia White. What on earth do you think you're doing? Thurman will never forget this. You've made people laugh at him, and he'll bully you cross-eyed on account of it.

"Good for you," Hazel whispers to me, and hooks her arm in mine.

"Hey, Audrey." I hear a familiar voice, and I find Virgil is right beside me.

"What lays on the bottom of the ocean and twitches?" he asks me.

"What?"

"A nervous wreck."

I try to laugh, but I can't get Thurman's mad red face out of my head.

Jewell Valley wins the game, and Daddy is a hero. I watch him go round the back of the schoolhouse with Arthur Rife, Lewis Viers, and Red Nunley. They prob'ly have a bottle of liquor stashed out there.

I walk through the camp toward home with Yvonne and Ruth Carol, also Virgil, Thurman and Ron Keith, and all the other kids. I can feel Thurman's beady little eyes on the back of my head all the way home.

8

At home Mommy has the zinc tub full of clean warm water. She has already took her bath, and now it's my turn. I go upstairs and get me some fresh things—a dress and some underwear and socks. Mommy lays out a towel and worshcloth for me, and pulls the curtain over the kitchen door so I can worsh by myself.

I sink into the tub and rest my head on the edge. I love the feeling of warm water on my back. Suddenly, from the other side of the curtain, I hear sounds like voices from a bad dream.

"Give 'em here, Olive!"

"Please don't take 'em, John Ed."

"I earned 'em! They're mine!"

I hear a noise that sounds like the table is knocked hard, so that it screeches across the board floor. A chair falls down.

I go under the water and hold my breath as long as I can. I can't hear much now. Just some muffled sounds.

Mr. Rochester and Jane Eyre are walking across the moor. They are deep in love. It's a clear spring day and the purple heather is blooming all around, and Pilot is running through it, chasing a rabbit—if they have rabbits over there in England. I bet they do have rabbits.

I can't hold my breath anymore. I come up and listen. There is not a sound. He is gone.

In the silence I can hear a baby crying from the other side of the house. Then the baby is quiet, and Mr. and Mrs. Church are talking with somebody. Their daughter must be visiting with her husband and babies. They prob'ly heard Daddy and Mommy fussing. By this time tomorrow everybody in the camp will know our business.

When I am worshed and dressed, I go to Mommy. She's at the table just staring at nothing. That dark point in the middle of her eye that's usually only a dot now looks like spilled ink over the blue part.

Yvonne is beside Mommy. Eleanor and Ruth Carol are on the floor, cutting out people from a Sears and Roebuck catalog.

"John Ed took the scrips!" Yvonne says to me. She always calls Daddy that behind his back.

"All of them?" I ask.

"Most of them. He only left a few."

We know without saying it what he is going to do with the scrips. He'll not buy food with them, that's for sure. He'll go to the company store and cash them in, and spend the money at the liquor store. That's what he'll do.

Mommy gets up and goes into the kitchen. I help her carry the bath water out the back door. We pour it over the little porch. It runs through the cracks and makes black puddles underneath. Then we take clean hot water from the stove, and put it in the tub. Yvonne and Eleanor go outside and get some cold water from the pump. When the hot water is tempered with the cold, the three little pigs climb into the tub together.

"What's the matter with Eleanor's eye?" I ask Mommy.

Mommy is soaping Ruth Carol's head and acts like she don't hear me.

"Is it a stye?" I go on.

"It'll be all right," Mommy answers.

"Do you want me to go and borrow some of that stuff from Mrs. Church?" I ask her.

"What stuff?"

"The stuff you borrowed when Daddy had a stye. That white salve."

"No, it'll be all right," she repeats, and I know she hasn't heard a word I said.

She rinses Ruth Carol's head with warm water.

When we are all bathed, dressed, and groomed, we eat a little supper of cold biscuits, applesauce, and peanut butter. Then Mommy gets sixty-five cents from her hiding place, and the five of us take off walking to the show. We go nearly every Saturday night. They run the same movies over and over, and they are real old, but we don't mind. Tonight it's Shirley Temple in something or other.

Me and Yvonne walk behind Mommy and Eleanor and Ruth Carol. I can see Mommy's hair is done up with bobby pins, two nice buns on each side of her for'd. Her shoes are resoled, run-over brown oxfords, and her dress is old, but it's clean.

And I know there's not a hole in Mommy's socks or in her underwear, 'cause she's not like some of the other women in the camp who pull things together with safety pins. She mends every hole and patches all the threadbare places in our clothes.

Mommy does not have lipstick or powder. Still she is pretty. I hope I look like her when I grow up, but I prob'ly won't.

Thurman and Ron Keith pass us running. I reckon they are going to the movies, too.

"Piggy! Piggy! Piggy!" Thurman squeals.

"Oink! Oink! Oink!" comes from Ron Keith.

At first I don't understand. I have never told *them* my nickname for Yvonne, Eleanor, and Ruth Carol. I wouldn't do that. I can call my sisters what I want to, but I don't like anybody else calling them names.

Then I glance over at Yvonne, who is frowning, at Eleanor with her puffy eye, and at Ruth Carol chewing on her dress tail. Oh . . . hh, now I know what it is. Mommy has plaited their hair in pigtails. She does that sometimes to keep it out of their faces.

Then Thurman stops and looks back at us like he just thought of something brilliant.

"The piggies and the skeleton girl!" he hollers, and both boys bust out laughing. Then they run on.

Skeleton girl!

I cross my thin arms over my chest. I look down at my bony knees. And my face grows hot with shame. *Skeleton girl* is ten times worse than *Little Audrey*.

"I can't stand them boys!" Yvonne hisses low under her breath. "They put me in mind of John Ed!"

Never thought of that before. But I reckon it's true. Little bullies grow up to be big bullies.

"Did Daddy hit Mommy again?" I whisper to Yvonne.

"He shoved her out of his way. She hit her hip on the table."

At the theater, we don't ask Mommy for stuff to eat. We know she's got only sixty-five cents. Twenty-five cents for her ticket to get in, and a dime each for the rest of us.

The floor in the theater is gooey, and my shoes and Mommy's make sticky, sucking sounds as we walk down the aisle. I'm awful glad I got on shoes now, 'cause it's nasty in here. My sisters are bare-footed.

The place is crowded and smells like not every-body had their Saturday baths. People are talking, children are whining, babies are fussing, and we have a hard time finding five seats together.

"Here, Miz White, you and your girls can slide in here," somebody calls to us.

It's Mr. Steele, and Mommy gives him a slight smile as she squeezes past him and Mrs. Steele, to the middle of the row. Ruth Carol is right behind her, then Yvonne, Eleanor, and me last. I sit down beside Mrs. Steele. She is eating popcorn. It smells so good.

"Where's Grace?" I ask her. Grace is their girl, and she is in my class at school.

"She's in here somewheres with Hazel," Mrs. Steele says.

I decide not to go looking for them. The lights will go down in a minute. Sure enough, the theater gets dark, and the newsreel comes on. It's all about the United Nations. Next Donald Duck waddles and quacks across the screen for about ten min-utes, and everybody laughs. The previews of coming attractions tell us that Van Johnson and Esther Williams will soon be starring in *The Thrill of Romance*, a movie that will tickle your funny bone and warm your heart. Oh, I hope I can see it!

Now the main attraction, starring Shirley Temple, comes on. It's real dark in here. And I'm thankful for that. You wanna know why? 'Cause as I sit here watching this sparkling little girl in her black patent leather slippers and lacy socks, hot tears start rolling down my face.

She is tap-dancing up and down a winding staircase. She has ribbons in her hair, and they bounce along with her yella curls as she moves. She flashes dimples and perfect teeth when she smiles. Her dress is short and full, and when she twirls round in it, you can see the ruffles on her little step-ins. She is the most adored child in the world. And I hate her.

9

I am dreaming about the day Daddy got home from the war. I dream it a lot, and it's always the same—the way it really was.

Mommy was out milking the cow she bought for us. It was a nice old cow. We called her Bess Truman. She would wander around in the hills till she was ready to be milked, and then she would stand out behind the house swishing flies and chewing her cud till Mommy went to tend her.

I was only eight, and I was reading a *Blondie and Dagwood* comic book in the living room. The three little pigs were upstairs making tents out of their sheets.

I heard a car at the front of our house, and when I looked out the window, there was Daddy climbing from a taxicab. He was handsome in his army uniform. He paid the driver, then came into the house, dragging a big green army bag. I stood there looking at him. I couldn't say a word.

"Well, if it ain't my little girl all growed up!" he said to me, and held out his arms. I went into them. He hugged me. He smelled like cigarettes and dirty hair, but not liquor.

I moved away from him. I was glad to see him, but . . .

No, I was not glad to see him.

That's right. I had a secret dread of this day the whole four months he was gone. 'Cause I knew when he came home, we would not have food on the table reg'lar anymore, and new clothes from the catalog.

"Where's your mommy?"

"She's out yonder milking Bess Truman."

Daddy laughed. "Doing what?"

So I explained about Bess Truman, and he laughed harder.

"Well, where's your sisters?"

I pointed to Eleanor and Ruth Carol, who were peeping over the stair banisters.

"Come tell your old daddy hello!" Daddy called to them, and held out his arms.

They came toward him slow, with their fingers in their mouths. Ruth Carol was only three years old then, and Eleanor was only four. Maybe they had done forgot who he was. He hugged them, and they just looked at him, like he was a stranger and they were too bashful to speak.

"Where's Yvonne?" he asked.

But nobody knew. I learned later she was hiding under the bed upstairs. She had not forgot who he was.

About that time Mommy came in the back door carrying a bucket half full of milk. When she saw Daddy, she dropped it, and it splattered all over the floor. Mommy and Daddy went into each other's arms and kissed, just like in the movies.

"No use crying over spilt milk," I remember Daddy said to her as he helped her clean up the mess. And that seemed awful funny to both of them. They giggled together like teenagers. It was the first time I had seen Mommy really laugh after Betty Gail died.

I dream of Mommy and Daddy settin' there at the table counting money in stacks. I'm sure that really happened. And it was real money.

Daddy had not seen even one fight in the war. In fact, he had been stationed in Texas. But he had learned how to win at poker. At the end, he had bet his last paycheck in a poker game and won big time.

I was so busy watching Mommy and Daddy together that I forgot about Yvonne, and suddenly there she was at Mommy's elbow, peeping around at Daddy. There were dirty streaks down her face where she had been crying.

"There's my Yvonne Marie!" Daddy said with a big old grin on his face. Then he took Yvonne on his lap and hugged her tight and kissed her tears away.

The rest of the day we were like a real family. We kept running back and forth to the store for good things to eat. Mommy and Daddy hugged and kissed a lot, and us kids took turns sitting on his lap. I thought maybe, just maybe the army had changed him, and made him stop drinking, and turned him into a real daddy. Oh, I hoped! I hoped!

"Are you on furlough?" Mommy asked him after while.

"Not exactly," Daddy said. "But the war is nearly over."

"John Ed! Did you go AWOL?" Mommy screeched.

"Hell no!" he said. Then he sighed a big long sigh. "All right, I'll tell you what happened. You know I lied when I signed up."

Mommy nodded her head. Yeah, everybody knew he lied. He didn't tell about having four children at home. The only reason he went was for that monthly check from the United States Army. It was more than he made working in the coal mine. We had just moved to Jewell Valley when he enlisted, but the coal company let the miners' families live here for free when their men went off to the war. Mommy had not minded a bit that he went, 'cause she would have allotment checks coming in the mail straight to her. She would spend it on things we needed instead of on liquor.

"Well, somehow they found out," Daddy explained. "They told me a man with four young'uns orta be at home with them, and they sent me packing."

"Oh," Mommy said.

"I reckon they're right," Daddy said. "I belong here with y'all."

Then him and Mommy kissed again.

In the evening he took his guitar from its hook on the wall in that storage place under the stairsteps. We had not bothered it the whole time he was gone, though we had wanted to pluck on it lots of times.

First he picked and sang "Froggie Went a'-Courtin'," and it made Mommy and Daddy laugh so hard their faces turned red, and they had to take time out to catch their breath, blow their noses, and say, "Oh, Lordy! Oh, Lordy!" over and over again.

Daddy explained that was the song he had sung to Mommy the first time he saw her up there on the top of Compton Mountain.

"There were eleven young'uns in that batch," Daddy said to us. "But your mommy was the prettiest and the brightest of 'em all. I got the pick of the litter!"

And they laughed some more. When they had

settled down some, Mommy said to Daddy, "I was reading Edgar Allan Poe from Uncle Hannibal's library, and you wanted to read it, too! Remember?"

"And you know what?" Daddy hollered at us. "Your mommy wouldn't let me borrow that book!"

"Well, it wadn't my book to lend," Mommy defended herself.

"We set up housekeeping in that li'l ole brown house down there close to the mines where I worked then," Daddy said. " 'Member that house?"

"Remember?" Mommy sputtered. "How could I forget? It was so little you couldn't turn around without bumping into yourself!"

Then Daddy played and sang all the war songs—"Open Door—Open Arms," "Over There," "I'll Be Seeing You," "We'll Meet Again," "The White Cliffs of Dover." We had heard them all on the radio, so we were able to sing along with him. Mommy never was much for singing, but she liked to listen. We sang for hours, until we were too tired to sing anymore. And Daddy carried us off to bed.

Oh, if only we could have gone on with that day forever! But it was a fairy tale. And the dream ends there. I wake up in the dark with a warm feeling. I go back over the dream in my head.

But I won't think about what happened after that. I won't think about Daddy going back into the mines. About Daddy trading Bess Truman for a wringer worshing machine that worked fine for a month, then blowed up. About Daddy picking up his old habits.

I sit up in bed and shake my head to clear it of bad thoughts. The moon is all the way full tonight. I look around at the drawings on the wall.

I hear a noise and look out the window. I can see everything plain outside, and there is Ernest Wimmer walking down the middle of the road in the moonlight. I know he is sound asleep. Ernest is older than me, but he's in my class at school. That's 'cause he's dumb as a coal bucket.

Thurman and Ron Keith usta pick on him all the time. But one day right in the middle of 'rithmetic, Miss Stairus said that Ernest Wimmer was a good boy with a good heart. And nobody picked on him anymore. It's like Miss Stairus had ordered it.

"Ernest!" I holler out the window. "Ernest! Wake up!"

He stops walking.

"Ernest!" I holler again.

Yvonne sits up in bed. "What's the matter with you?"

"It's Ernest walking in his sleep," I tell her. "I gotta wake him up."

"You're not supposed to do that," Yvonne says. "It might scare him into a heart attack."

"Well, I'd druther cause a heart attack than have him walk out on the big paved road like he did last winter. He might get runned over."

Ernest stands still in the road, like he's waiting, listening.

"Ernest!" I yell one more time.

He does a slow turn and looks toward my window.

"Go on home, Ernest!" I tell him. "Git back in the bed!"

To my surprise he throws up a hand at me, and starts walking back to his house up the road. I watch him till he's out of my sight. Then I look at the moon and think.

Sleepwalking is a strange thing, you know it? You go through all the motions of being awake, but you're really asleep. Sorta like what Mommy does, I reckon.

10

On Sunday afternoon the camp is quiet. We are all sitting on the front porch, listening to music from the radio in the house, all except Daddy. I reckon he's laid up drunk somewheres. He didn't come home last night.

Georgia Hale comes walking by with her baby, Mary Ellen. People say Georgia's husband quit her and went off somewhere. The mining company told her she would have to move, but she's got no place to go. People who can afford to part with food give it to her, but they say she can't go on like this. I wonder what she'll do.

The gossips say she is looking for another miner to marry her, so she can stay in the camp. They say that's why she puts on fresh clothes every day and walks up and down the road. She's trying to get a man.

Today she has her hair done pretty, but there's dandruff all over her dark blouse. It just ruins her looks. Mommy won't stand for dandruff. She puts castor oil on her scalp when she gets it.

"How old is she now?" Mommy suddenly calls to Georgia.

Me and my sisters look at Mommy. We're surprised as all get-out to hear her voice so bold and normal.

"Seven months old," Georgia Hale says.

She walks close to the porch and turns the baby around so we can see her better.

"My last baby was seven months old when she died," Mommy says. "She would've been four years old on the seventeenth day of this month if she had lived."

I count the days in my head. The seventeenth was last Monday, a week ago tomorrow. I forgot the baby's birthday, but Mommy didn't. So that's why she's been floating around the house, carrying her whole life in her eyes. Betty Gail's birthday musta been the trigger this time.

"Her name was Elizabeth Gail," Mommy says real soft.

"What a pretty name!" Georgia Hale says.

"We called her Betty Gail."

"That's nice, Miz White."

"Mary Ellen is a pretty name, too," Mommy says.

Then Georgia moves on, and Mommy goes back into her head.

Not long after, a taxi pulls up to our house, and out steps Daddy and Granny and Poppy. I am so glad to see Granny and Poppy, I run to meet them.

"Audrey!" Granny cries, and puts her arms around me. Then she holds me at arm's length. "Let me look at you!"

Daddy goes up on the porch and into the house without a word. Poppy pays the taxi driver and tells him, "Come back for us at midnight."

"Young'un, you've fell off so bad!" Granny says to me. "Why, you're nothing but skin and bones."

She makes me feel ashamed.

"And I just can't get used to them glasses!" Granny goes on. "You don't look like yourself. You still got one gray eye, don'tcha?"

I nod. She peeps under my glasses.

"Hidy, Olive," she says to Mommy at the same time. "How you been?"

We go up the steps to where Mommy's at.

"I'm all right," Mommy says. "How're you, Edna?"

"Can't complain, I reckon."

She plops herself down beside Mommy, pulls out a Lucky Strike, and lights it. Granny smokes more than anybody you ever saw. She turns to Yvonne, Eleanor, and Ruth Carol and blows the smoke out in little rings.

"And how are you girls doing?"

They don't answer. Granny don't really care for the three little pigs, and they know it. They just stand there next to Mommy, watching the smoke rings. Poppy comes up the steps with his fiddle slung over his shoulder.

"How's my girls?"

We all have smiles for him.

"How are you, Zachary?" Mommy says.

"I'll do, I'll do," he mumbles.

Daddy pokes his head out the door. "Olive, don't we have nothing to eat in this house?"

"I was going to fix salmon patties for supper," Mommy says.

"I don't want no salmon patties!" Daddy sputters. "What else we got?"

"I'll buy us a chicken," Poppy says, pulling money out of his pocket. He turns to me. "Audrey, run down to the store and get one."

That was exactly what Daddy wanted Poppy to say. I know Daddy's tricks pretty good.

"And I need another pack of Luckies," Granny says. "Give her fifteen cents more, Zachary."

Poppy hands me a two-dollar bill. "Might as well get some treats for my girls, too," he says.

"Oh, boy!" I say. "Can I pick out anything I want?"

"Why not?" Poppy says with a laugh.

"Why does *she* get to go? Why can't I go, too?" Yvonne says in a pouty way.

"Go on, then," Poppy says to her. "And you better pull that lip back in before you step on it!"

Me and Yvonne set off for the store, and Mommy goes into the kitchen to start supper.

At the store, we get the fattest chicken we can

find. The butcher wraps it in waxy white paper and lays it by the cash register while we look at the goodies. I buy us some Coca-Colas. We'll get a penny back on each bottle when we return them.

Yvonne gets some little boxes of peanuts to put in our Cokes. The elves who pack the peanuts place a coin in the bottom of each box. You never know what you are going to get, a dime or a nickel or a penny. Most times it's a penny, but Ruth Carol got a dime one time. It like to tickled her to death.

"Don't forget Granny's cigarettes," Yvonne says.

We buy a pack, then we get enough Bazooka bubble gum, Tootsie Rolls, Mary Janes, and penny suckers to take up the rest of the money.

On the way home we run into Grace and Hazel. They are out trading comic books. Grace is a girl who grows so fast, her clothes always look like they drawed up in the worsh. She's gonna be a woman before me and Hazel get started.

"You got any funny books to trade?" Grace says to me. She is just being polite. She knows dern well we don't. Sometimes we find one that somebody has pitched out, but for the most part we don't ever get any funny books.

That don't stop us from drooling over what they got—*Superman*, *Little Lulu*, *Sheena*, *The Green Hornet*, *Captain America*.

I am jealous.

"Hey, I heard a new Little Audrey joke," Grace says. "Wanna hear it?"

"Is it about her getting captured by cannibals?"

"No, it's about her boyfriend jumping off a building."

"I don't wanna hear it anyhow."

"I do," Yvonne says.

"Well"—Grace takes off—"Little Audrey had a boyfriend, see, and he was begging her to marry him, and she wouldn't.

"Finally he said to her, 'If you don't marry me, I'll throw myself off the highest building in town.'

"Still she wouldn't say yes. So shore enough, that poor jilted boyfriend climbed up there onto the top of the hotel roof, and he jumped off. Splat! It made the awfullest mess you ever saw on the sidewalk.

"And Little Audrey just laughed and laughed, 'cause she knew all the time that the hotel was not the highest building in town."

Yvonne and Grace and Hazel all laugh together.

"See you later!" I say, and stomp off, leaving the three of them standing there in the road looking after me. I know I'm grumpy, but I just don't get it. What's so doggone funny about Little Audrey jokes anyhow?

"Hey, Audrey, wait a minute!" Hazel hollers at me.

I stop and turn around. "Whadda you want?"

"I wanna ask you something."

"Then ask."

"What does it mean when somebody says, 'It goes without sayin' '?"

I am exasperated. I roll my eyes.

Hazel comes up closer to me and whispers, "I was trading funny books outside Thurman and Ron Keith's house, and I heard them in there talking about you."

My heart starts pounding of a sudden, and I clutch my grocery pokes close to me. "Oh? What did they say?"

"Well, Ron Keith said to Thurman, 'Audrey White made you look bad at the ball game. You gonna make her sorry, ain'tcha?'

"And Thurman said back to Ron Keith, 'That goes without sayin', don't it?' "

11

In the living room, Daddy and Poppy have dragged the lamp table to the middle of the room and pulled up three chairs to it. They are fixing to play a game of poker while Mommy cooks supper.

Daddy is shuffling the cards. Him and Granny and Poppy are all drinking something from coffee cups. Yeah, it's bourbon. I've smelled it often enough, I orta know.

Yvonne takes the chicken to Mommy.

Poppy is showing Ruth Carol a trick with his hands. It's not much of a trick. He used to show it to me when I was little.

"Here's the church. And here's the steeple. Open the door. And here's the people!"

Ruth Carol laughs. "Do it again! Do it again!"

I hand the pack of Lucky Strikes to Granny. She takes the old pack and pushes it into my dress pocket. "There's one left in there," she whispers to me.

Wow! A whole cigarette all for me!

"I want some candy!" Eleanor says, and tries to take the poke of goodies from me. I hold on.

"Me too!" Ruth Carol whines. "I want some candy, too!"

How come she's gotta whine like that? Can't she just say things normal?

"No candy till after supper!" Poppy lays down the law, and everybody is disappointed.

He takes the poke from me and sets it up on the top of the radio. Eleanor and Ruth Carol slouch out to the porch. I slip outside and go to the toilet, where I hide my cigarette in the rafters.

Soon we are at the supper table eating fried chicken and mashed potatoes with real margarine to melt in it, biscuits and boiled cabbage, too. We act like we never had food before. It tastes so good.

After supper we go into the living room again,

all but Mommy. She cleans up the kitchen. I take the poke full of candy off of the radio. Yvonne goes digging into the peanuts to see what kind of coins are in them. But today we get only pennies.

Daddy fetches his guitar from its hook. Poppy sticks his fiddle under his chin. And they commence playing and singing. They sound good together. Then we all join in—tapping our feet and smacking and chewing and swigging and singing all at the same time.

"Here's a song," Poppy says to us, "that reminds me of your daddy when he was about knee-high to a sweat bee." And he begins to sing.

"Climb upon my knee, Sonny Boy
Though you're only three, Sonny Boy . . ."

Poppy's eyes are misty. Drinking liquor always makes him tender-hearted. Then he starts telling us a story about when Daddy was a little five-year-old boy and got in trouble. We've heard it before, but it's still funny.

Poppy was going to whoop him, but Daddy ran outside. When Poppy come out looking for him,

Daddy hid in the chicken house. Poppy called and called, but Daddy didn't answer.

Then Poppy went to the chicken house and said, "John Ed, are you in there?"

No answer.

He repeated, "John Ed, are you in this chicken house?"

And a tiny scared voice came back. "Ain't nobody in here but us chickens!"

We all laugh so hard. I look at Daddy, and I can't imagine him being a little boy five years old. That's about the age of Virgil's brother, Earl.

Mommy has moved into the room like a shadow. She is smiling at Poppy's story. I can't imagine her as a five-year-old girl either. But she was. She really was. And she laughed and cried and played hopscotch.

What happened to them kids? Are they still somewhere inside these big people? Lost and wondering what happened? Crying 'cause they can't find their way out? I don't want to get lost like that.

We sing "Bonaparte's Retreat," "Down Yonder," "Long, Long Ago," "Billy Boy," "Dem Golden

Slippers," "Beautiful, Beautiful Brown Eyes," "Wildwood Flower," "Sweet Betsy from Pike," and nearabout every other song we know. All but one. We don't sing "Froggie Went a'Courtin'."

As usual, Mommy don't sing, but Granny tries. She takes a puff off of her Lucky Strike, then sings a line, then takes another puff and sings another line. Then all of a sudden she starts in to coughing. She coughs and coughs and coughs.

Daddy and Poppy stop playing. We all look at Granny. She goes on coughing. Her face turns red. She looks like she can't get her breath good. Mommy gets her a rag, and Granny coughs into it. Stuff comes out of her throat and into the rag.

I have to look away so I won't throw up my supper. Ruth Carol and Eleanor watch Granny like she's a really interesting thing to see. Yvonne is purely disgusted.

Finally Granny settles down and goes back to breathing normal.

"Lordy mercy," she says over and over. "Lordy mercy."

Daddy starts picking the guitar again. Poppy plays the fiddle. We sing some more. We eat more candy. And Granny lights up another cigarette.

12

It's Monday morning, and Mommy does her best to get me moving, but I have a hard time leaving my bed. When I finally do, Yvonne and Eleanor are already gone to the schoolhouse. Ruth Carol is still sleeping. She's been rooting around trying to find a dry spot in the bed. Now she's curled up on a pillow.

Anyhow, it's nice to have the kitchen to myself. Mommy has heated some water for me. So I pour it in the worsh pan. I clean out my eye boogers and take a bird bath.

"I saved you a piece of chicken for dinnertime," Mommy says to me when I come out of the kitchen. "I put it in this poke with a sidemeat biscuit."

So she *is* worried about my weight. I eat the sidemeat biscuit on the way to school.

I don't like to walk past the coal tipple. It's right beside of the road, and when you look up at it, it seems as big as King Kong against the sky. Sometimes I imagine that it will reach down and grab me.

Being by myself today, I hear something that I wouldn't ordinarily hear with all the other kids around. I stop and listen good. It's the squealing of hungry baby birds. I look up at the tipple, and I am thrilled at the sight. That mommy bird has built her nest right there in the elbow of one of the metal pieces that holds up the tipple!

About ten feet off the ground, it's tucked in there pretty good, so the weather is not likely to reach it. At the moment the mommy is dropping stuff into four little stretchy squealy mouths.

I don't know what kind of bird it is, 'cause I don't know one bird from another. But I'll have to say that's one dandy nest she has pulled together out of strings and sticks and scraps.

I step closer. Right there is a scrap of cloth that I'll declare come from our house. Mommy used to have a blouse made out of it, and then she tore it up for quilt pieces. And now here's a piece of it in a bird's nest!

They are saying the Pledge of Allegiance when I go in my classroom. I stop just inside the door, put my hand over my heart, and recite with them.

Miss Stairus is a different flower every day. Today she's a buttercup in her yella dress and yella hair. I can't get enough of looking at her. As I walk past her to my desk, I notice she smells like cinnamon, and she's wearing sandals on her tiny white feet. Her toenails are painted pink. I wisht I had me some sandals and pink nail polish.

Instead of fussing at me for being late, Miss Stairus shows me her dimples. She's sending me this secret message: there are worse things than being late.

In Miss Stairus's room all the desks are in short rows facing each other instead of in long rows facing the front of the room, like in your ordinary classroom. There are thirty kids in my class, and they come from about a dozen different hollers around Jewell Valley.

I put my poke with the fried chicken in it inside my desk. I will have it to look forward to all morning. Across the way I can see Ron Keith and Thurman and Hazel. Hazel gives me a little wave. Ron Keith and Thurman give me an evil grin. Grace and Ernest and Virgil are on my side of the room.

"Arithmetic first!" Miss Stairus says to us, and we take out our 'rithmetic books and paper and pencils, too.

My pencil is getting real short, and I'm near-about out of paper. I will have to tell Mommy today that I need more. I dread telling her. But now I remember it's the last week of school. Maybe, just maybe I can make this pencil and these few pieces of paper last till Friday. I'll not sharpen the pencil unless I really have to.

Miss Stairus goes and sets down in an empty desk. This is a thing she does a lot. Pretends to be a schoolgirl right along with us. Today her place happens to be between Ron Keith and Thurman. They look at her with worship in their eyes. Here is the one thing I have in common with these rascals, and all the other kids in our class. We idolize this fairy-tale princess. We would gladly be her slaves.

After arithmetic, we study geography and history. The next thing I know, it is recess time. An hour and a half has passed that quick! Today it's the boys' turn to go out first, while the girls stay behind and straighten up the classroom before we go outside. Tomorrow it will be the boys' turn to stay behind.

We have everything all neat in no time, and I go looking for Virgil. I find him between the playground and the woods, standing over a small pile of dirt. In one hand he is holding a dead bird. He is supervising its burial for a group of first-graders. Ain't that just like Virgil?

The little kids are standing around him trying to cry. Eleanor is in the group. I notice the stye on her eye is better today. It was not a bad one. Her sweetheart, George Elmer McGaffy, is standing beside her. I hang back until Virgil is finished reciting some words from the Bible.

"Glory be to the Father and to the Son, and into the hole he goes!"

With that he dumps the dead bird into the grave he has dug. He rakes the dirt over it with his foot. He pats the kids on the head one at a time and says goodbye to them as straight-faced as a preacher. Then he walks to me.

"Here they come," he whispers. I know he is

talking about Thurman and Ron Keith. "I'll handle it, Audrey. Just go along with me. Okay?"

"What do you mean?"

"Just trust me, and go along with what I say."

I nod as Thurman and Ron Keith come up beside us, grinning.

"Okay, skeleton girl and prissy boy," Thurman says. "You ain't gonna get out of it! Let's set a time right now!"

"What about tonight?" Virgil jumps in headfirst. He is smiling.

I think Thurman and Ron Keith are so surprised, they don't know what to say next. They look like players in a movie where the projector just quit on them.

"Can't y'all come tonight?" Virgil says to them.

They still don't speak.

So Virgil turns to me. "How 'bout you, Audrey? Can you come tonight?"

"Tonight? Why . . . sure, Virgil. Tonight's fine."

Ron Keith is the first to come to his senses, and he gets right in Virgil's face.

"What time?" he says through clenched teeth.

"Midnight, natur'ly!" Virgil says. He is still smiling. "Okay?"

"You won't do it!" Thurman says. "You little prissy boy!"

"*I* will be at the tank at midnight," Virgil says, pointing to his own chest and emphasizing the *I*. "How 'bout you?"

Thurman bristles like a dog fixing to fight. "You think I'm scared?"

"No!" Virgil comes back. "I don't reckon you got any reason to be scared, have you? I ain't scared a bit."

Thurman stares at him for a long time, then turns to me. "How 'bout you, skeleton girl? I bet you're scared, ain't you?"

"No, I'm not scared." I say it brave enough, but I swallow hard.

"You orta be scared," Ron Keith says.

Thurman laughs. "Yeah, you orta be real scared. I ain't forgot your smart-alecky remark at the ball game."

I shrug.

"All right, then. Midnight at the tank." Thurman grins.

"I'll declare, I can't wait!" Virgil says. "I've been thinking about it all weekend. It'll be a lot of fun!"

I can tell by the expressions on Thurman's and Ron Keith's faces, they don't quite know how to take Virgil. I don't hardly know myself.

When Mrs. Boyd, the principal, rings a big cowbell, we have to go in. Me and Virgil lag behind the others going back into the classroom. Ahead of us we see Thurman and Ron Keith put their heads together. Then they turn around to look at us, and bust out laughing.

Virgil grins and waves at them. "I got a plan," he says to me low under his breath. "Don't worry, Audrey. I'll take care of everything. You'll see."

13

During reading class, we are deep into a story about Africa when it gets to be Virgil's turn to read out loud. Virgil is a pretty good reader, so I am surprised when he stops at the word *jaguar*.

Miss Stairus pronounces the word for him.

"Oh, I know the word," Virgil says, "but something just popped into my head. You wanna know what it was, Miss Stairus?"

Miss Stairus smiles at Virgil and waits.

"Well, I was thinking how glad I am that we don't have any jaguars around here, and I'll tell you why. Tonight I am going up on the hillside at midnight, and as much as I like animals, I would not want to run into one of them critters in the woods in the middle of the night."

Thurman and Ron Keith shoot a sideways look at each other.

Miss Stairus's face takes on a puzzled look. "At midnight?" she asks Virgil. "What on earth for?"

"I am going to climb all the way to the top of the water tank!" Virgil says, and actually claps his hands together. He has this big dumb grin on his face. "Then I'm gonna walk around the edge at the top of the tank!"

I look at Miss Stairus. All the color has drained out of her face.

"Won't that be fun, Miss Stairus?" Virgil goes on.

She does not answer.

"It's gonna be more fun than a barrel of monkeys!" Virgil says, and looks around at all his classmates. "Don't y'all think so?"

The room is quiet.

"No, Virgil," Miss Stairus says between clenched teeth. "No, I do not believe it will be fun. It will be very dangerous!"

The smile fades from Virgil's face. "No foolin'?" he says.

"Absolutely!" Miss Stairus's voice finds strength. "In fact, I have never heard of anything so . . . foolhardy!"

Nobody knows what *foolhardy* means. But we can guess.

"Is that right, Miss Stairus?" Virgil says with so much innocence, I am impressed.

"Did somebody put you up to this, Virgil?" Miss Stairus sounds kinda stern. Now the color is coming back into her face.

Ron Keith and Thurman slide way down in their desks.

"Oh, no, ma'am. I thought it up all by myself," Virgil lies. "I like to dream up interesting things to do that nobody ever did before."

"Well, I forbid it. Do you understand me, Virgil?"

Virgil hesitates. "So you think it would be a stupid thing to do, Miss Stairus? Really stupid?"

"Ordinarily I would not use that word," Miss Stairus says real soft. "But yes, it would be . . . it would be extremely stupid!"

"Oh . . . hh . . . hh." Virgil draws the word out. "Well, I don't want you to think *I'm* stupid, Miss Stairus. If you say it would be a stupid thing to do, then maybe I'll dream up something else to do. Something that's *not* so stupid."

I can see Miss Stairus's whole body relax, and she smiles at him.

"Promise me?" she says real sweet.

Virgil nods his head.

"You know, Virgil, I would not want to take this up with Mrs. Boyd . . . or with your parents," Miss Stairus goes on.

Virgil is quick to say, "I promise!" He crosses his heart with his right hand. "Cross my heart, hope to die, stick a needle in my eye!"

"What about the rest of you?" Miss Stairus asks us. "Will you promise me, too?"

"We promise, Miss Stairus," everybody choruses.

Miss Stairus looks us over one by one slow and careful, while we wait to hear the praise that we know is coming.

"You are all so wonderful!" she tells us. "I would not trade even one of you for a pot of gold!"

14

For two days I have been in a new place in my head. A good place. I have not been in Jane Eyre's world even once. 'Cause my hero is in this world. He said he would take care of everything, and didn't he, though? Ron Keith and Thurman don't know what to do next. To displease Miss Stairus would be their worst nightmare. And they can't look me in the eye.

But it's Wednesday now, and in our house there's nothing but beans left to eat. We don't even have any cornmeal or flour for bread. And there's nary a scrip or a piece of change to be found.

Daddy don't say one word while we eat our beans. After supper he's on the couch reading Zane Grey, and the rest of us go tiptoeing around.

I decide to get out. I will go and visit with Hazel. She has a swing on her front porch, and we sit out there in the twilight. We swing and talk. Swing and talk. It's nice. I stay till it gets dark.

Then Hazel's mommy comes out and says, "It's time to come in, Hazel. You better run on home now, Audrey."

So I walk back toward the house. It's cloudy tonight, and the air feels heavy. There is only one star in the sky that you can see. But you only need one star if it's as bright and sparkly as this one. One star in a cloudy night sky. Maybe I could write me a poem.

I feel all dreamy as I set down on our front porch steps and whisper, "Star light, star bright, first star I see tonight. I wish I may, I wish I might, have the wish I wish tonight."

Then I cross my fingers, squeeze my eyes shut, and wish real hard.

"What did you wish for?" a voice comes out of the shadows on the porch.

I jump up quick. It's Daddy. Now I can see his

cigarette glowing red in the dark. He has his feet propped up on the banister that runs across the front.

My tongue is tied in knots. "I . . . I . . ."

"Come over here and tell me," he says. And he pats a chair beside him.

I walk over there and set down.

"Well, what did you wish for?"

"For . . ."

"For what?"

"To . . . to gain back all the weight I lost when I was sick."

"Oh," Daddy says.

We are quiet now, and you can hear the frogs croaking down in the creek.

"Did your granny say you're too poor?"

I shrugged. "It's not Granny. It's some of the kids at school."

"Do they tease you?"

"Yeah."

"Do they call you names?"

"Yeah. Skeleton girl."

We go back into the silence. The quieter we are, the louder the frogs croak. One old bull sounds like he might be having a nervous breakdown.

Daddy speaks kinda nice and soft. "You'll gain that weight back, Audrey."

Fat chance of me gaining any weight when we never have enough food in the house. But I just think that. I don't say it out loud.

"What else would you wish for?" Daddy says. "If you could have anything in the world, what would you wish for?"

I shrug. "Oh, I don't know. Maybe . . ."

"Maybe what?"

"For us to live better than we do."

He does not say anything. I sit beside him and don't speak. He looks at the sky and takes another puff off of his cigarette. That's when I remember the one I hid in the toilet. Maybe I'll smoke it tonight. I'll need a match.

It seems like Daddy is done with me, so I stand up and stretch.

"Guess I'll go to bed."

"Night," he mumbles.

I go in the house and find the three little pigs at the eating table. Using scrap paper, Eleanor is practicing her printing, and Yvonne is tracing a map of Virginia from a book. Ruth Carol is trying to color her fingernails with a crayon. She only has a red crayon and a blue one left out of her box of eight.

I go into the kitchen. Mommy is at the stove mashing up the last of the cooked soup beans into a mush.

"What are you doing?" I ask her.

"What?"

"Why are you mashing up beans?"

"I'm going to make bean patties for breakfast."

"Huh?"

"They will be good," she says.

I don't believe her.

"You'll see," she says. "It'll be all right."

I try to look through the window at the darkness outside, but I see only my own reflection. It's deep dark now. Do I really want to go out there to the toilet and smoke my cigarette? I glance at the box of matches on the stove ledge. No, Mommy will see me. If I take a match, she'll know what it's for. She won't like it.

So I go to bed.

15

On Thursday morning I am woke up by the rain slashing against my window. It's still dark outside, but I can hear Mommy trying to get Daddy out of the bed. He is grumbling, and she is pleading.

"Come on, John Ed, you know you gotta get up and go to work."

"All right! All right!" he hollers at last. "I'm up. Now shut up!"

I see Mommy go past my door and down the stairsteps. She is dressed already. She always gets up early, even on Sunday. She gets lots of work done before the rest of us open our eyes.

I hear Daddy stumbling around. I know Mommy has laid out his work clothes and socks and shoes. Downstairs she will have his dinner bucket ready. I wonder what she put in it today. Bean patties?

I think of Daddy walking to work in the rain. Checking into the office down there below the tipple. Riding the tracks way down into the belly of the mountain on one of them little mining cars they have. Crawling around in the dark with his carbide lantern strapped to his helmet. Digging coal out of the bitter black earth all day long. Stopping long enough to eat his bean patty.

And this great rush of pity nearabout swallows me.

Oh, Daddy, I'm so sorry you have to work in that place, in the dark, in the cold. I wisht I could go to you and hug your neck, and tell you how much I love you.

My eyes are as blurry as the windowpanes. It is a mean day for May. It should not be like this. I need to sleep some more. But every time I try to fall back into my dreams, I see Daddy digging coal in the dark mine. I know I will think about him all day.

The bean patties are not too awful bad. We each

have a small one for breakfast and another tucked into a poke for dinnertime at school. I can imagine me and my sisters sneaking out our bean patties and trying to eat them without the other kids seeing them. But I've seen kids bring worse things to eat for lunch.

When school lets out, it's still raining outside. It has been a depressing day, and tomorrow is my last day in Miss Stairus's class. I don't want the school year to end.

And I don't want to go home. I think if I hang out at Hazel's for a while, her mommy will give us a snack. But Hazel runs ahead of me with Grace. Maybe she has started to like Grace better than me. But that's okay. I like Virgil better than her.

I walk with him in the drizzle. I don't look up at the birds' nest as we go by the tipple, 'cause I don't want to give away their hiding place to mean boys like Ron Keith and Thurman.

Virgil cheers me up saying funny things. For a few minutes I forget about Daddy in the mines, and about going home to where there will be nothing to eat for the next twenty-four hours.

But now I am home, and I have to go in. I walk slow through the living room. Something smells good. Mommy and the three little pigs are setting there at the table with soup bowls full of something. Am I dreaming? No, this is real food. But where did it come from?

"Come on and eat, Audrey!" Ruth Carol calls. She has something all over her face. So it's not a dream. That's real food on the runt piglet's face. It looks like beef stew!

I set down, and Mommy places a bowl full of the stuff in front of me.

"Where did it come from?" I say before cramming my mouth full of beef and potatoes and carrots and peas all in a thick brown gravy. It's so good, I can't hardly believe it's real.

"I was saving it for a rainy day," Mommy says, and glances out the window.

She says no more. Just sets back down and finishes eating her own stew. We all eat for a few minutes without talking.

"It has carrots in it," I say. "Where did you get carrots this time of year?"

"The stew came in cans," Yvonne says. "Four cans."

This is such an odd thing, I can't figure it out.

"Where did it come from?"

Mommy goes into the kitchen and comes back with one of the cans in her hand. She is reading the words on the can.

"It came from St. Louis, Missouri," she says.

Me and Yvonne bust out laughing. Mommy smiles at us. I look for the daydreams roaming around behind her eyes. But they are not there today. Somehow she has managed to pull herself out of that dark place once more. Whatever it was, she is over it—at least for now.

I eat all I can hold, and don't ask her any more questions. But I feel something mysterious and magical in the air.

"Ain't you gonna save some for Daddy?" I ask as I watch Mommy dip up the last of the stew for us.

Mommy shrugs. I take that to mean no. Daddy can manage.

When our tummies are full, Mommy takes the dirty dishes into the kitchen, and we keep on setting at the table. The rain lets up. The sun tries to come out. It feels good in here. Cozy.

Suddenly Mommy comes back into the room and grabs the flyswatter off its hook. She looks around at all the walls and corners of the room. Now I hear the buzz. Mommy hates flies. When she starts chasing one down, she won't quit till it's dead.

I decide to help her. I jump up and grab a *Farmers' Almanac* to swat the fly. Me and Mommy start chasing it. Yvonne and Eleanor and Ruth Carol jump up and run around, too.

"Shh . . . hh," Mommy says suddenly, and we all fall still to listen for the buzz.

There it is! We go running toward the window. We trip over each other. We start giggling. We pounce on that fly, but it's Mommy who kills it dead against the windowpane.

Smash! Oooo . . . oo. It makes a mess.

Mommy cleans it up, then turns to us with a pleased look on her face.

"Kill a fly in May, and keep a thousand away!" she declares.

We gather round her then and hug her like she's just come back from a long trip. She hugs us back.

Then she announces, "Guess what we are going to do?"

"What?" we screech.

"We are going to bake a cake!"

"A cake?" I say.

"A cake?" Yvonne echoes me. "We don't have stuff for making a cake!"

"Who says we don't?" Mommy wants to know, and props her hands on her hips.

We don't answer. We just watch her and wait.

She flings open a cabinet door and looks inside. She takes out a little bottle of vanilla flavoring and an almost empty can of baking powder. She sets them on the table.

"There, that's all we need."

We stand looking at her. Has she lost her mind?

"Except . . ." She puts her chin in the palm of her hand. "Except for flour. That's all we need—a cup and a half of flour."

She takes two cups from the cabinet and turns to Yvonne.

"Yvonne, take these cups and go to Mrs. Wimmer and ask her if we can borrow a cup and a half of flour."

"Okay," Yvonne says. She is excited. She takes the cups and runs out the door.

"And that's all we need," Mommy repeats. "A cup and a half of flour . . . and . . . oh, yes, sugar. We need sugar."

She pulls out another cup and hands it to Eleanor. "Eleanor, take this cup, and go to Mrs. Steele's, and tell her we need to borrow a half cup of sugar."

Eleanor's eyes are shining. "Okay, Mommy." She takes the cup and goes out the door.

"And that's all we need," Mommy repeats. "Except for milk. We need a half cup of milk."

She hands a cup to me.

"Mrs. Mullins?" I ask.

"That's right," she tells me. "But we shouldn't all be out there at the same time borrowing stuff. Wait till your sisters get back. And while you are gone, I will go over to get an egg from Mrs. Church."

"What about me?" Ruth Carol whines. "What can I do?"

"Why, you have the most important job of all!" Mommy says.

Mommy takes the last cup from the cabinet. "Short'nin'! You can go and ask Mrs. Nunley to put two tablespoons of short'nin' in this cup. But not right now. Wait till Audrey gets back."

But Ruth Carol snatches the cup and runs out the door. She is too excited to wait.

"Wait!" I call to her, but it's too late.

"That's okay," Mommy says.

"What kind of cake will it be, Mommy?" I say to her.

"What kind?" She thinks for a moment. "Why, it's a Jewell Valley cake, natur'ly!"

And we laugh a little. Then we cry a little.

So here we stand, me and Mommy, huddled together in this nest she has pulled together for us from strings and sticks and scraps. And the two of us laugh and cry, and laugh and cry.

16

It is only a little cake and we have no icing for it, but a Jewell Valley cake is real good anyhow. We are setting around the table eating it when darkness falls on us. Daddy did not come home from work. He has done this before on Thursday evening. It seems like some weeks he can't wait till Friday night to get drunk.

He gets liquor from his buddies. He'll stay out all night and miss work tomorrow. He might even stay gone Saturday and Sunday, too. We never know what to expect from him when he goes on a real big drunk.

"Tomorrow y'all have only a half day of school,"

Mommy says. "So when you come home, I'll have a great big old hot dinner waiting for you."

"Are you going to pick up Daddy's paycheck?" I ask her.

"Yeah, I'll go to the office and get it tomorrow morning early," Mommy tells us. "It will be short, since Daddy probably won't be going to work tomorrow."

The last day of school is always lots of fun. Every class gives a fruit shower for the teacher. Our class is no different. That means we are supposed to bring a piece of fruit to give to Miss Stairus. She will go home all loaded down with mostly apples, but a few oranges and bananas, too.

Of course, me and my sisters don't have fruit for our teachers. But we are not the only ones. There are lots of kids who can't bring fruit.

"Oh, thank you, thank you," Miss Stairus says to us. "You are the best class in the whole wide world."

We look at her with everlasting love in our eyes and in our hearts.

At recess, Miss Stairus asks for only one person to stay behind and help her straighten up the room—and I'll bet you can't guess who that person is. Me! I am so tickled, I jump up and start worshing the blackboard before the others are out the door.

"Sit down, Audrey," Miss Stairus says to me when we are alone.

I wonder why she tells me that? I set in the first desk beside her, and look at her, and wait. She is a pink rose today.

"I received three bananas in my fruit shower, Audrey," she says to me.

I nod and smile at her.

"And I hoped you might eat one of them for me."

She takes the biggest banana from the pile of fruit on her desk and hands it to me.

I feel my face go hot. So she knows. She knows. But I take the banana. I lay it down in front of me.

"Go ahead and eat it," she says. "I know you love bananas. You said so in one of your stories, and I can't eat three of them before they go bad."

She takes a banana and starts to peel it for herself. Then I pick up my banana and peel it, too. I eat it as slow as I can. It is so . . . ooo good. The taste lingers in my mouth for a long time.

On our way home from school, Hazel runs

ahead of Grace and catches up with me and Virgil.

"Did your daddy come home last night?" she whispers to me.

I shake my head.

"Mine neither," Hazel says with a sigh.

We just look at each other.

"And I hear tell Lewis Viers didn't come home either," Hazel whispers some more.

"They are prob'ly all together somewheres," I say.

This has happened more than once in our memory. But that's the way it is. We don't often talk about it.

After Hazel goes into her house, me and Virgil walk on together. I walk fast 'cause I know what's waiting at the house.

"Hey, Audrey!" he hollers at me as I go up our front steps. "Where do you find a one-legged monkey?"

"I don't know. Where?"

"Right where you left him!"

I give him a big grin and a wave, and go inside.

Mommy has cooked the best dinner of fried Armour Treet meat, canned peas, and boiled potatoes with cheese melted in them. We have milk to drink, and a big old pot of rice pudding for dessert. It has raisins and cinnamon in it.

Mommy has spent all of Daddy's paycheck on food. There is enough to last us maybe even longer than a week. But right now I can't eat another bite.

Mommy leaves the leftovers on the table and covers them with clean dishcloths. She tells us to try and eat all the food before we go to bed, so it won't go bad.

Now it's time to go around the neighborhood and pay back the ingredients we borrowed for the Jewell Valley cake. My sisters were eager enough to borrow the stuff, but now they grumble at paying it back. They help me do it anyhow.

After that, we gather round Mommy on the front porch, and she tells us a story about when she was a little girl up there on the top of Compton Mountain. They were poor, but they always had plenty to eat because they raised their own food and canned it, and dried it, and salted it so that it lasted all year long.

We don't have a place to raise our own food here in the coal camp. One time Mommy planted some tomatoes behind the house, but the plants were trampled down by people walking back there.

We hear the sound of a motor, and watch as Mr. Church come up the road with his son, Dwight, in Dwight's old black Ford. They stop in front of our house, and get out.

"Hidy, Miz White!" Mr. Church calls to Mommy.

Mommy throws up a hand at him.

Mr. Church walks over to our porch. "I seen your brother Warner down at the Pilgrim Knob Store. And he said to tell you that he will drive up here Sunday morning and take you and your girls up on the mountain for Decoration Day, if you want him to."

"Oh, yeah, he knows we want to go," Mommy says, and smiles at our neighbor. "Thank you, Mr. Church."

"He said for y'all to be ready around ten o'clock," Mr. Church goes on.

Then him and his boy go into Mr. Church's side of the house.

Oh, goody, now we got something to look forward to. We love going up on the mountain, especially for Decoration Day. There will be dinner-on-the-ground at the cemetery, and we will see all our cousins. There's nearabout a hundred of them. But I exaggerate. Twenty or thirty maybe.

We keep running into the house to grab another bite to eat from the table. It feels good to eat all you can hold. It is such a nice day, I want it to last longer. But it ends just like all the other days. It is over and we are in bed before you know it.

And Daddy does not come home.

17

On Saturday, Mommy fixes us a big breakfast. It is drizzling rain, so we don't go outside. We mope around the house while Mommy worshes clothes and sweeps the floors. We don't talk about it, but we are all thinking about Daddy, and wondering when he'll be coming home, and how drunk he will be. If he's real bad drunk, somebody will haul him in the house and dump him. And he'll sleep it off. He'll be grumpy when he wakes up.

If he's halfway drunk, he'll be hateful. He'll be mad as an old wet hen that Mommy spent all the scrips on food. He'll rant and rave about that. He might even hit her. I hope he don't hit her.

If he's just a little bit drunk, he'll go around joking with us. But we don't much like his jokes. Maybe he'll try to flog our fannies with a dish towel. He thinks that's funny. But I got news for him. It stings like fire. Sometimes it leaves a red mark.

At noon we have liver cheese sandwiches with mayonnaise and lettuce. They are good. Then we each have a banana. We dip them in peanut butter.

The baseball game is at Oakwood today. I know 'cause I heard Mr. Mullins holler to his wife that he is going to Oakwood to see the ball game. I wonder if Daddy will pitch. He might not be able to. He might not even show up.

In the evening we take our baths, eat some canned soup, and go to the show. Mommy has saved enough change for that, and for popcorn and Orange Crushes, too. *The Thrill of Romance*, with Van Johnson and Esther Williams, is playing. It is good. Mommy loves it. She laughs at everything.

On Sunday morning Uncle Warner comes promptly at ten o'clock. He has borrowed an old rattletrap pickup to haul us up the mountain. First

Mommy carries out a poke full of books she has borrowed from Uncle Hannibal and puts them in the back of the truck. She will return them today and pick out some more.

Then she carries out the potato salad she has made for the dinner-on-the-ground, and climbs up in the front with Uncle Warner. Me and Yvonne and Eleanor and Ruth Carol are tickled to ride in the back.

It is the prettiest day you ever saw. All the clouds are gone, except for a few little white puffs over the hilltops. The wind blows in our faces, and we laugh so hard.

We ride out of Jewell Valley and onto the big paved road. There are houses built on the hillsides and down at the edge of the river. Some of them have neat, grassy yards. There are barns weathered to a slick gray finish, and chicken pens and hog pens.

There are tidy gardens all along the roadside, and you can see the first slender green cornstalks peeping up from the ground. You can see tomato plants propped up with stakes to keep them out of the dirt, and over yonder I see some green bean vines. The cucumbers are pickle-sized. And the little beds of spring lettuce are so green and pretty.

We go up the Loggy Bottom road almost to the top of the mountain, and then we have to get out and walk. But it's not far. We come out of the woods, and suddenly there's the sky in front of us. The top of the mountain stretches out nearly flat, with cow pastures, houses and yards, gardens, and the cemetery.

Besides all the dead Comptons under the ground, there are live Comptons and people who have married Comptons walking above the ground. They move around and visit with each other. They are happy to see us. Some of them are old and some of them are young. But most of them are somewhere in the middle, like Mommy.

First we pick wildflowers and decorate the graves. Grandpa Whitton has put a chair beside the grave of Grandma Gertrude. He sets there and talks to people. He has a long white beard and looks exactly like Father Time. We are bashful with him.

We play with our cousins in the woods and pastures. We know Aunt Ruby's kids the best 'cause we see them the most. They are Peggy and Doris and Roger. We have a good time together.

Aunt Ruby is Mommy's younger sister. She always looks pretty. Today she has on a nice blue dress with butterflies on it. Her hair is done up in curls. And she smells good.

We have dinner-on-the-ground around noon. Mommy talks to her kin and laughs a lot. Her face sparkles. After we eat, everybody goes to Uncle Patton's house. It's just a little bitty house, so most of us stay in the yard. The strawberries are ripe and growing everywhere. Aunt Clara tells us to pick all we want. We pick them and put them in a poke to take with us.

Along toward evening, Mommy tells Uncle Warner we had best go home. But first we stop by Uncle Hannibal's house. Now we are heading toward home all loaded down with books, and leftovers from the picnic, and wild strawberries.

Daddy is not on the front porch. When we go in the door, we stop and listen. We don't hear a thing. He is not anywhere downstairs. Mommy goes upstairs to check, but he is not there either. I am glad, but where is he? He still is not home when we go to bed.

18

W ake up, Audrey."

Somebody is shaking me. I look up and make out Aunt Ruby perched on the side of my bed. I blink and rub my eyes.

"Aunt . . . Aunt Ruby?"

"Yeah, it's me," she whispers. "Are you awake?" She is crying.

"Whatsa matter?" I ask her.

"It's your daddy, Audrey."

I set up and look at Aunt Ruby. "Whatsa matter?" I repeat.

"He . . . he's . . . dead," she says, and her voice breaks.

"No he's not," I contradict her. "He's just off drunk somewheres. He'll be home drek'ly."

"He's dead, Audrey," Aunt Ruby says, looking me square in the eye. "He was in a car wreck."

I am so aggravated with her. Why does she say such a thing to me?

"Where's Mommy?"

"She's downstairs. She needs you to keep the girls up here and out of her way for a while."

I look at my sisters in their bed, still asleep and dreaming. Maybe I am asleep and dreaming, too.

"They're asleep," I say. "How come you're here so early in the morning?"

"I come to help your mommy. She's tore up pretty bad."

I lay back down. Now my ears have heard Aunt Ruby's words. Daddy has been killed. Daddy is not coming home. He is never coming home again. But my heart has not heard it yet.

I look at the ceiling. Rain has come in over there near the door. It has made a big brown spot. When did that happen? I wonder if Mommy has seen it. She don't like leaks in her roof.

"I want to go back to sleep," I say to Aunt Ruby.

Without another word she goes out. I see her standing there at the top of the stairsteps for a second. Then she grabs on to the banister with both hands and walks down slow.

I don't go back to sleep. I get up on my knees and look out the window. It's going to be a nice day.

I see Mrs. Wimmer coming up to our porch. She is carrying a plate of something with waxed paper tucked in around the sides. That's what people do when there's somebody dead. They take food to the house. Then it must be true.

But I don't have to think about it. I get up and put on some clean clothes. Then I go and see what Mrs. Wimmer brought us to eat. It's sausage and biscuits. They are good. Aunt Ruby is at the table. She does not ask me why I didn't stay upstairs like she told me to. She looks at me with watery red eyes. I eat my sausage and biscuit.

Mrs. Wimmer is in the living room talking to Mommy real soft. I can't hear what she is saying. I go back upstairs. Yvonne is standing at the top. I feel like hitting her.

"Why is Aunt Ruby here?" she asks me.

"Daddy is dead," I say to her, and push her back to her bed. She fights me all the way, but I am bigger than her.

"He is not!"

"He is so, and I heard it first, not you!"

Yvonne tries to smack me, but I hold her at arm's length. She's such a priss.

She hollers at me. "I'm going to tell Mommy what you said!"

We glare at each other. Then I step aside, and say to her, "Go ahead, little piggy. Go tell her."

Let her find out for herself.

I look at Eleanor and Ruth Carol still asleep in their bed. How can they sleep like that?

Yvonne comes back eating one of the biscuits with sausage stuffed in it.

"The car went off the road and over a mountain," she says with her mouth full.

"Who told you that?"

"Nobody. I just heard them talking."

"Who was talking? Who else has come in?"

"Mrs. Wimmer and Mrs. Mullins and Mr. Steele and somebody I don't know. It's a man. He's wearing an army suit with a badge on it."

She means a uniform. The only uniform Yvonne

has ever seen was Daddy's army one. But I know that lawmen wear badges.

"You are so ignorant!" I say to Yvonne. "You don't know a lawman when you see one."

Yvonne finishes eating and licks her greasy fingers. Then she pulls a cardboard box out from under her bed. It's where she keeps her clothes. She rummages around and brings out a pair of shorts to put on.

"Mommy won't let you wear shorts today," I say to her.

"Mommy won't care," she says.

She's prob'ly right. Today Mommy will be far away from us. She won't see or hear us. She will prob'ly be away for a long time.

19

Through the day all kinds of good things are brought in for us to eat. Bread and meat and stews and vegetables and cakes and pies and I don't know what all. Me and my sisters eat all we can hold. Other people eat, too. There's enough for everybody. Somebody takes a plate to Mommy, but she just picks at it.

About two o'clock, Granny and Poppy come to the house. Poppy's face is like a Halloween mask: old and gray and wrinkled up. And it don't move a bit.

Granny is crying and smoking, crying and smoking. Her eyes are pouring tears. Her face is red. I try to hug her, but she pushes me away. She smells like liquor and tobacco. She sets down at the table where all the food is at, but she does not eat.

It's late in the day when the undertaker comes in a big long black car and brings Daddy to us. Some people move our furniture around in the living room, and find a place against the wall to put the casket. The undertaker opens up the top half of the casket lid. I walk over and look at Daddy. There he is laid out in a nice suit. I wonder where he got that suit. His hands are folded over his tummy, and his yella hair is worshed and combed neat. He looks like he's in a peaceful sleep.

Granny comes in to see him, but she can't stand it. She starts to moaning and hollering. Somebody helps her to a chair.

Mommy goes to the casket then. She is quiet, but I can see that her lips are moving. She is saying something to him. I don't know what. Maybe it's very personal.

Yvonne stares at Daddy, then goes away. Eleanor and Ruth Carol won't go near him. They stand by the front door. Eleanor sucks her thumb, and Ruth Carol chews on a sprig of her hair that's just long enough to reach her mouth.

The undertaker has brought chairs, and they are scattered around the house and out on the front porch. More and more people come in. They look at me and my sisters. They talk in whispers, but I hear some of what they say.

"All girls? No boys?"

"That's right. Four girls."

"I didn't know that."

"There usta be five girls. The baby died a while ago."

"They all look like Olive, don't they?"

"Except for the oldest one. She looks like John Ed."

"Poor little girls."

"What in the world is Olive going to do?"

"I'll declare I don't know."

"Her people ain't able to help out."

"I know. They got little enough for their own selves."

"Maybe Edna and Zachary can help some."

"Maybe."

I listen, but I feel like they are talking about somebody else. Then again I think I am in a dream.

Aunt Nancy has to come all the way from

Roanoke, so it is after dark when she gets here. She goes straight to Mommy and hugs her tight. Then she sets about cleaning the kitchen. If not for all the people, she would be cleaning everywhere. Aunt Nancy is a take-charge kind of person, and she can't stand dirt.

It gets later and later, and I fall asleep on one of the undertaker's chairs in the living room. The heavy smell of carnations wakes me up, and I see Mommy asleep in a chair beside Daddy's casket. It must be midnight, and people are still here, all over the place. They act like they are having a party. I wonder why they don't go home. Can't they see how give out Mommy is?

But they don't notice. They are too busy visiting with each other. I tiptoe up the stairsteps to bed. I find my sisters asleep with their clothes on. Aunt Ruby washed the pee out of their sheets early in the day, and Aunt Nancy has scrubbed the floor. It is still wet in places. I fall into my own bed. What a strange, strange day it has been. I wonder, when I wake up in the morning, if it will go on like this, or will I find it was all a real bad nightmare?

20

When I get up, I put on my clothes, then go down to eat some more. People are still all over our house, wandering in and out. Somebody's baby is crawling around on the floor. She wants me to pick her up, but she's got hockey in her diaper. I escape out the front door.

Hazel and Grace and Virgil come up the road and stare at me. I walk out to where they're at. I don't know how to act with them staring at me like that.

"Does it feel awful, Audrey?" Hazel asks me.

I shrug. "Where y'all going to?"

"My daddy was with him," Hazel says.

"With who?"

"With your daddy when he got killed."

"Oh."

"But he can't even talk about it. He went to bed and won't get up. He said he is not ever going to drink another drop of liquor in his life. Arthur Rife was driving, and his car was pretty well ruint. It was him and my daddy and your daddy and Lewis Viers, but nobody else was hurt much, just your daddy. They said his head was—"

"Where y'all going to?" I know I'm repeating myself, but I don't want to hear any more about Daddy getting killed.

"Nowhere," Virgil says. "You wanna come along?"

We all walk together up the road. They keep on looking at me sideways.

"You know what my daddy said?" Hazel says.

She can't help herself, I reckon, but I wisht she would just shut up.

"He said when they were down in the mines on Thursday your daddy said he thought his family would be better off without him."

With a pang I remember me and Daddy talking together on the porch on Wednesday night.

"He said that this past Thursday?" I ask Hazel.

"Yeah, the last day they worked together before they took off on their drinking binge."

"It's the first day of June." Virgil tries to change the subject. "How come you're not barefooted, Audrey?"

That's right. I forgot what day it was. I think about taking off my shoes, but somehow it don't seem right to go barefooted today.

"Mama says y'all will have to move," Grace says.

She didn't have to tell me that. Everybody knows only miners and their families live at the coal camp. I think of Georgia Hale, walking around with her baby, scared and desperate, and I wonder where in the world we will go. We won't get scrips anymore either. We will have to have real money. Where will we get real money?

Daddy said we would be better off without him.

Of a sudden Virgil reaches over and pats me on the back. Why did he do that? I don't know why, but it brings up a fullness in my chest. My throat and jaws ache. My breath is coming too fast. I turn sharp on my heel and head back home. I can feel their eyes on me all the way.

Once inside the door, I see her—Miss Stairus! I

know now it will all come out of me. But you know what? It's okay. I go to her, and she folds me into her arms like a great bird wrapping a chick under her wings. Deep choking sobs come up out of me, and I can't stop them. I cry and cry all over her pretty dress. She is a violet today. She holds me and says nothing. Nothing at all.

I don't know how long I cry, but when I peep out at the world again, I see that she is crying, too. That's how Miss Stairus is. She shares everything.

She stays with me for a long time. It must be hours. She keeps her arm around me while she walks around my house and looks at how we live. She even goes up the stairsteps to my room, and sees the slop jar. I am so glad Aunt Nancy has emptied it. Miss Stairus runs her hand over a single butterfly that Yvonne or Eleanor has added to the Sheetrock drawings. She still does not say a word, but she cries like her heart is broke.

21

It's suppertime now, and Miss Stairus is gone. I don't want to be around all these people anymore, so I slip out the back door and head up the hillside toward the water tower. The kids have drove a path into the ground walking from the camp to the tank. I don't think anybody will be there at this hour. Most people are home eating. Now I am alone and haunted by my last conversation with Daddy.

"If you could have anything in the world, what would you wish for?"

"For us to live better than we do."

I could have said a lot of things besides that. Why did I say it? It must have hurt his feelings. The tears are coming down my face again. Ahead, the water tank is a big silver blur against the sky. I set down beside an old stump.

I remember one time when he was just drunk enough to be in a good mood, and he brung us little black pistols made out of sweet wax gum. You could pretend-shoot with 'em for a while, and then you could chew on 'em.

And I remember one time . . . it was Christmas . . .

"Hey, it's Little Audrey!"

And there's Thurman and Ron Keith coming toward me. Of all the people in the world, it would have to be these two who find me like this. I stand up and turn away from them. I take off my glasses, and wipe the tears on my dress tail. But they walk around me and look right in my face. My eyes must be all red and puffy, and my nose is stopped up with snot. I have to breathe through my mouth.

They don't speak for a moment. Then Thurman says, "You look different without your glasses."

I don't know what to say or do. I glance down at

my dingy socks and old wore-out brown shoes. They're awful. Maybe I should go ahead and take 'em off.

"Can I try 'em on one time?" Thurman says.

"Yeah, me too," Ron Keith says.

I jerk my head up.

"What?" I am plumb bewildered, 'cause for a second I think they want to try on my shoes.

"Your glasses," Thurman says. "Can we try 'em on?"

"Oh." I look at my glasses clutched in my hand. I hand them to Thurman. "Be careful with 'em. They costed a lot."

"Okay."

Thurman puts the glasses on and turns to Ron Keith. "How do I look?"

Ron Keith thinks about it, then says, "Smart. They make you look smart."

"Do they?" Thurman struts around a bit.

"Whew!" he says, and takes them off. "Well, they make me *feel* dizzy. Do they make you dizzy, Audrey?"

"No, they were made for my eyes, not anybody else's."

Ron Keith takes the glasses from Thurman and

places them on his own nose. He glances around at the trees.

"Everything's fuzzy," he says. Then he takes them off and hands them back to me.

"Thanks," he mumbles.

"Yeah, thanks," Thurman says.

I don't know what to say to them, so I put my glasses on and start to go back down the hillside.

"Hey, Audrey!" Thurman calls after me.

I stop and glance back over my shoulder.

"Your daddy was a good pitcher," he says.

"Yeah, he was," Ron Keith agrees.

22

Daddy was buried on a beautiful spring day. I watched as they lowered the casket into the ground and started covering it up with dirt. But I didn't feel bad about that 'cause I knew Daddy wadn't there.

I don't know where he is, but that body he used to live in is empty now—as empty as that cocoon a butterfly leaves behind after wiggling out of it.

Now it's near the end of June, almost a month since the funeral. The people are gone back to their own lives. The eating table is normal again. That sweet, sickening smell of carnations has faded.

Me and my sisters are also back to normal, except for the bickering. We don't do that much now. I reckon we'll get back to it in time, but for now the quiet is like a solid thing in our house. You can just about touch it when you come in the front door. And it's there all through the night.

Virgil and his family have gone back to Kentucky. They left early one morning before anybody else in the camp was up. But he said goodbye to me the night before, and he gave me his address so that I could write to him. He promised to write back.

"And don't worry, Audrey," was the last thing he said to me. "You're a real smart girl. You'll always have that."

And I believe him.

Outside, the world goes on. The birds and katydids sing like they do in pretty weather. The children jump rope in the road and play hopscotch and Round Town and May I? and Red Rover and hide-and-seek. They wade in the nasty creek. The miners come home black with coal dust, and you can't tell one from another. So it's a reg'lar summer to everybody else. But for me and my family? Well, I can tell you, nothing will ever be the same again.

When Aunt Nancy was here for those few days, Mommy sat with her at the table, and they drank a lot of coffee together and talked.

I heard Aunt Nancy say to Mommy, "Olive, I want you and your girls to come to Roanoke to live with me until you can find a little place of your own. I think I can help you get on at the casket factory where I work. If not, then there's other things to do in Roanoke. It's not like here, where a woman can't get a job."

Mommy didn't say yes right off, but her face lit up. I figured she never dreamed she would be going out into the world to become a working woman, but I could tell by her expression that maybe it was a thing she might like to do.

Then Mommy told Aunt Nancy that we are getting a thousand dollars from the life insurance the mining company carried on Daddy. That is a lot of money, and it is not in scrips.

"And the Social Security check will come at the first of every month," Aunt Nancy said to Mommy. "Twelve dollars for you, and twelve dollars for each of the girls. Add that to your paycheck, and you orta be able to take care of these girls in a proper way."

Finally Mommy said to Aunt Nancy, "I can't think of a better plan."

I listened to this, but I wadn't sure if I believed it or not. Could it be true that things might work out for us?

I know that Mommy is afraid, but she is brave. Me and my sisters are nervous, too, about going to a new school in a new place, especially a big town like Roanoke. But you know what? I'm like Mommy—I can't think of a better plan right now.

The mining company wants us out of here as soon as possible. So tomorrow we are leaving Jewell Valley and moving to Roanoke to live with Aunt Nancy until we can find a house of our own. I daydream about our permanent house. I hope it is white.

Tonight Mommy fixes us a nice supper, and after we eat, she says to us, "Girls, I want to tell you something."

She is looking right at us with no dreamy or faraway look in her eyes. It's surprising, but I'm awful glad.

"Things will be different in Roanoke," she says. "You will meet all kinds of people, some good and some bad. Nothing will be the same as it is here.

But don't let that worry you. Just keep in mind that you are as good as anybody."

We watch her face and listen solemnly.

"And I want you to remember your daddy. There's no need to dwell on his bad habits," she went on. "Just remember the good things about him, the good times we all had together."

Then she hugs and kisses each one of us. "It'll be all right," she says sincerely.

On the way to bed, I stop by Mommy's room to look at myself in the mirror, and I smile. Yes, this time I believe Mommy. It'll be all right.

As I am leaving Mommy's room, I see where she has packed up her few things in a box, and on the top is that picture of all of us with Betty Gail in the yard. I pick up the picture and look at it.

And there she is, the sweet little thing. She would be four now if she had lived, and she would be moving with us to Roanoke to live with Aunt Nancy. I wonder what she would be like.

I feel so much tenderness in my heart that my eyes start to burn, and tears spill onto my cheeks.

"What are you doing?" It is Mommy standing in the doorway.

I brush the tears away real fast and put the picture back where I found it.

"Nothing," I say.

I start to walk past Mommy, but she puts her hand on my shoulder and stops me. I look into her eyes.

"You are old enough to remember it all," she says real soft.

I nod. "I remember real good."

Mommy goes on looking at me.

"I miss her, too," I say, and my voice breaks.

Then Mommy takes me into her arms. She holds me for a long time as together we grieve for this precious little soul who was with us for such a short while.

I feel better. Lots better. And I think . . . maybe, just maybe, I will not be haunted anymore by cries in the night.

23

I wake up in the wee hours of the morning. I feel strange. I want to jump out of this bed and do something. I don't know what. I can't go back to sleep.

I think of the water tank up there in the woods. I look out the window. I can see a part of it. The only scary thing about it is the idea of walking around the top with all that deep water below you in the dark.

It's spooky, like the inside of the mines. I bet Daddy was scared in there. We have all heard stories about explosions and cave-ins. Just about everybody in the camp but us has had a family member to die in the mines. Mommy's oldest brother, Samuel, didn't die in the mines, but he caught a lung disease from the coal dust. He died the year I was borned. Mommy said he was the best boy that ever lived in this world.

I look at the tank again. I bet if you climbed up just about three-quarters of the way to the top at the right time, you really would see the most wonderful sunrise from that point.

I wisht the daylight would come, so I can get up. Now I know what I'm feeling. It's my good health returning. That's what it is. I knew it when I looked in the mirror last night. My face was plump again, and I could see the roses coming back into my cheeks.

The sun will be up soon. Yes! I will do it right now. It's my last chance. I will go and climb just high enough to see the sunrise over the hills yonder to the east. And while I am in the woods, I will smoke the cigarette that's still out there in the rafters of the toilet.

I get out of bed and put on my dress. I am real quiet. I slip into the kitchen and take a match from the stove ledge. Then I go outside, put my shoes on, and get my cigarette from the toilet. I walk up the path real fast.

I stop at the foot of the tank, and look toward the top. Yeah, I will climb just far enough to see the sunrise. But I have time to smoke first.

I set down on the ground and strike my match on a rock. Then I take the first puff. I cough. I smoke and cough, smoke and cough. And it comes into my head that I must look like Granny setting here smoking and coughing. That's all she does. Smoke and cough.

And you know what? If it's one thing I'm sure of, it's that I don't want to look like or be like Granny, and that goes for Poppy and yes, Daddy, too.

Now, don't get me wrong. I will always love and remember that little boy in the chicken coop who said, "Ain't nobody here but us chickens."

I smile. Yeah, I'll put him away in my heart in the same place where I keep Betty Gail. And I will remember that boy who sang "Froggie Went a'Courtin' " to his girl. Surely that boy who started working in a coal mine when he was seventeen dreamed of more. And I'll remember the man who came home from the war.

But I won't remember the drunk. I'll forget him.

There is one person—no, two—no, three people that I am sure I want to be like when I grow up. The first one is Miss Stairus, in the way her heart is big enough to hold all of the valley. The second is Virgil, in the way he uses his brain to solve his problems. And the third, my mother, in the way she does the best she can do no matter how miserable she feels. Yes, I will call her Mother now. It suits her, and it sounds so fine.

I crush the cigarette into about a dozen pieces in the black dirt. Then I get up and climb the tank. I climb almost to the top, but not quite. I breathe in the cool morning air.

Now I am so glad I came up here. 'Cause way out there beyond the horizon I can see a new day ready to be born. And it's a good day. It's full of people like Miss Stairus and Virgil and my mother. And beyond that I imagine all the tomorrows lined up, just waiting for me.

As the sweet daylight hits my face, I can't help

smiling. Little Audrey just laughed and laughed, I am thinking, 'cause she knew all the time, in spite of everything, it's a good world out there.

I have never helped Mother enough. I will go home now and do all I can for her. She'll be tickled. I'll help the three little . . . I mean . . . my sisters, too.

Sure, I'm smart enough to realize we will still have problems. I don't expect everything to be easy. But now somehow I really believe that me and my sisters will manage to grow up to be good people and make our mother proud of us.

I go down the steps of the water tank real careful, then walk the path into the coal camp for the last time.